THE LOST DIARIES
of
JIM MORRISON

COMING OF AGE
BOOK I OF III

EDITED BY:

Marshal Lawrence Pierce, III

Wasteland Press
the literary renaissance
a Published In Heaven Book

Wasteland Press

Louisville, KY USA
www.wastelandpress.com

the literary renaissance

Louisville, KY USA
www.tappingmyownphone.com
www.literaryocean.blogspot.com

a Published In Heaven Book
for the literary renaissance

The Lost Diaries of Jim Morrison
edited by Marshal Lawrence Pierce, III

The hour of departure has arrived, and, we to go our own ways.
I to die and you to live.
Which is better God only knows.

-Aristotle

Believe me! The secret of reaping the greatest fruitfulness and the greatest enjoyment from life is to *live dangerously*.

-Friedrich Nietzsche

C'mon, baby, light my fire.

-Jim Morrison

Dedicated to the memory of my loving Grandmother,
Julia Tomczak.

for John Rooney whose constant love, support and care
brought me further then even I would have realized alone.

INTRODUCTION

I have tried to do my best to put into words my story, the story of how these diaries came to be. For, I knew that someday, someone, anyone, would for his sake wish to know.

Yet, it is not a story one easily forgets. It is imprinted upon my memory like an image appearing upon a photograph. For, I am unable to forget her, forget her story, forget the night we met. I can only relish that odd feeling I had sitting with her for those few minutes which felt like hours, feel like years now.

Please know and believe me when I tell you that what you will read is not fiction. And, no matter what anyone says or claims, these words are the ones to believe; they are the literal truth. Her story is indeed true. Let the many others who will call this work fiction, do so. But, please do not be led astray. For, yes, skeptics with critical eyes will have no heart. Thus, let them not steal yours, steal your soul away. Let your heart make the decision as to the validity of these diaries. Give not unto their power over you, I implore you, please.

Know that I have worked from the original manuscripts of these diaries spilling both blood and sweat over the years, pained over the many pages which were indecipherable, as they were once left in the rain and were stored in moist conditions. Diligently, I copied the original pages word for word for your eyes to behold, for you who love and adore him too, keeping his memory alive.

Except for the spelling of a few words and some corrections with grammar, these words, phrases, and slang are all exactly as he chronicled them in these diaries. Added by me were the diary entry numbers; I am hopeful that they will make the reading of his writings a bit easier to follow.

Clearly, there was no joke, no fraud, no prank perpetrated upon me in my meeting with her. Make no mistake, the diaries were all in his hand, as an expert in handwriting analysis helped me to see this fact from some original papers of his written while he was a student at UCLA and FSU.

Sometimes, I wonder the reason as to why she chose me of all the journalists in the city to give these diaries to. I still vacillate over, "why me?" Now, I know what an honor it was to be given the diaries. And, she can confirm no thought of mine as I realize that she is now dead. It's kind of like a lonely feeling of fame inside me.

So, for you who seek, wonder, and desire to know, here is how his diaries came to be, how they came to me:

When I first heard about them, there was no doubt, it was an incredible story. I was not sure if what I was hearing was a joke, a wish, or, the actual truth. Yet, her voice was so desperate, almost frantic. She spoke softly, ever so clearly though. As we chatted at first on the phone, I simply wanted her story to be true perhaps? So, I agreed to meet her. She proposed to giving me his words. The lost diaries of Jim Morrison. James Douglas Morrison of, *The Doors*.

What first amazed me was that she claimed that Jim Morrison had not expired in a Paris bathtub. But, rather, he "survived his death," lived after the famous "passing" in 1971. Simply, as I listened more and more to her I began to think I was dreaming, or, this must be some sort of prank. Yet, her voice was so real, so passionate, as she spoke of him. Maybe some actress of sorts, but, who would desire to pick me out of a crowd and jerk me around? I had few friends. Well, that was not true, I had no friends. No fans, thus, no one could have traced my whereabouts from free-lance ghost writings in obscure newspapers or magazine. So, in reality who could this be but her?

What the hell was going on? I was not ready for her, for her story, for such an allegation. It was preposterous. My head ached from a 'bout of gin and cigarettes when she called.

Though the clock said, 245 P.M., it was still too early in the day for me. I almost hung

up. But, it was her last pregnant pause, when her voice cracked, and I heard her tears amidst the sniffles and coughs. They were real. No acting, no joke. She was indeed telling the truth.

She spoke of this cancer which was consuming her body, and, before it would touch her mind she wanted his words not only to be preserved, but, to be shared. I agreed to our meeting in the Village in a ratty hole of a joint where Bob Dylan first heard Joan Baez sing her songs of peace and protest over the Viet Nam war.

As I walked into the night club, I glanced towards the curb where Dylan first met Baez, hitting on her daughter. The great mother, the open-minded liberal, snubbed him, pushing her girl into the cab fleeing into the abyss of New York's concrete maze of the rich and the famous, the haves and have nots. I sneered at the bouncer at the door as I threw my cigarette onto the ground and walked inside.

The smell inside was disgusting. Stale beer. Old air. Smokey lights, the oily darkness hurting my eyes. Seediness was once part of my past. Now, I felt that I was way too old for such trivia, such filth. But, it was my idea to meet here, this place seemed appropriate for the hand off of one legend's words in pen, where other legends once sang in voice.

I looked for her, seeing no one I imagined her to be in this slum. She gave me no description of herself, only saying, "you shall know it is me when you see me." Another riddle? I rubbed my eyes, ordered a vodka tonic from a whore of a waitress who stood behind the sticky bar. I could not really hear this waitress when she offered me some ecstasy over the rap or rave music from their D.J. I only shook my head, "no."

Kids, zombie-like, lingered everywhere, touching everyone, clawing even at me. But, they were only aware of their own presence, unaware of the place's past. After all, Viet Nam had been lost and Ginsberg was dead. The mirrored ball insulted me most. Next, was the drink's taste.

I stood, leaning against the bar looking for my contact. Cheap glasses constantly clinked and clanged accompanying the music's beat, or, what some referred to as music. It was bad!

With the United States, nowadays, winning desert wars before they began, there

were no more protests, nothing more to inspire them. They only had music which lacked depth. But in it, one only heard noise. Nothing more, nothing less. The provocative in the realm of ideas had been stripped from their young minds. I reflected on my youth as I stared at this new generation of rebels, though rebels without a cause.

Now, punks only sprayed furs with cans of paint believing they were saving the world. Shit, not even some dumb animal was saved by them. So pathetic. I scoffed, took a sip of my drink when I heard it......her cough.

Where the hell did it come from? I could see nothing blinded by strobes and colored lights, some lousy disco shit. Where the hell was she? In fear of losing her I pushed against the wasteland of humans. Now, I was the frantic one. I continued seeking her out. Then, at a small corner table lost in a cloud of smoke, her own, I saw her. She nodded. Indeed, it was her.

Through her small French mouth, her two front teeth were exposed and brown from years of nicotine. I moved in closer, nodding back. She extended me not her hand, but, rather, a pack of cigarettes, one partially pulled out, mine I supposed. I took it, sat down and glanced away from her withered face as she gave me a light.

"So you made it? I wondered if you would," she said in that unmistakable accent of Paris. Her eyes were those of the Mona Lisa. A tall straight back only the Eiffel tower could rival. We sat quietly, motionless, at first. My discomfort finally broke the air, "I had no choice but to come, though, your claim, is, is....."

"Too hard to swallow?"

"Yes, exactly," as I began to laugh. She followed my lead.

"Fine, then, believe what you want."

"No, that is not what I meant, I mean, not what I mean. I meant....." I could see she was upset.

"Save it," she smarted off to me, looking away. But, where was the booty? Or, was I to learn this was some idea of some old college friend's joke?

Then, from something under the table, I think a bag, she pulled them out. Three books bound in dry crumbling leather, all the pages inside yellowed, many pages hanging outside of the book, too. A mess held together by rubber bands. She placed them on the table with an almost trancelike reverence.

By now the musical beat had egged on my already subtle headache. My head throbbed. I wanted to grab the mess and run, get out fast. She coughed and choked. I offered her my drink, she moved her head quickly, meaning, "no." She then pushed the books in front of me.

"So, how do I know that these are even real," I pleaded with her somewhat, "how do I even get in touch with you?"

"You don't," she growled with wide open eyes.

I began to remove the rubber bands. She touted, "No! Not here!"

She went on clearing her throat.

Truly concerned, I asked, "but, what if.....is he still alive? Now? For, I have been to the grave in Pere Lachaise in Paris, damn, even his parents had laid his memory to rest." Her eyes spoke loudly as she peered at me, almost meanly. I stopped rambling. I mixed my drink with some crappy paper straw all soft and soggy and took my last sip of the warm drink.

As I watched her sit and gaze at the crowd, I noticed that the last few years had not been good to her. I began to stare at her in some kind of a farewell tribute. Once, she was very beautiful, one could easily see that in her perfect jaw-line. Looking at her once soft skin under dried cracked makeup she made me believe that she was too good for Morrison, she was so much better than him. Even now he would not deserve such desperate elegance.

I imagined that beneath her black clothes were brightly colored sundresses which once danced, wine in hand, happily, in Provence. That under her cheap wig, once, long auburn hair flowed and blew briskly in the cold winds off the coast of Brittany, she holding her fur collar up keeping her neck warm.

Shit! All of a sudden I realized that she had throat cancer. She continued to cough, smoke and cough. Suddenly, I envisioned her in a coffin, no mourners, no flowers, as she began to cough so hard tears welled up in her eyes. "Can I.....?"

"No..." She signaled for me to leave now, almost crying in pain. I could not help but wonder of how an all-loving god could allow her to exist in such agony in her last days upon the earth. What was she being punished for? Loving Morrison?
"You live in Chelsea," I said.

"How did you know?" Finally, I got her to smile. So pure her look; she carried herself with such grace and charm, even at the end.

"How did you, rather, why did you call me, and......?" Finally, she had completely shut me out. Her mission was over. Her life, complete. She could die in peace. I would immortalize her in his words. Lighting up another cigarette, coughing incessantly, she hailed the barmaid with a nervous wave of the hand. I began to leave thinking that I had never learned her name.

I grabbed the books, soon to be acknowledged as diaries, and said good night to her as she continued her far away glance. Running the gauntlet in a growing mass of mankind's carnage, I left the place. Never to return. Never to see her again.

The words which follow are his story.

Marshal Lawrence Pierce, III
New York, New York
2002

DIARY ENTRY #1

Not that dead after all. She comes in, doesn't knock, starts up with some French. I'm like, "hey, slow it down, babe! Fucking talking like a rattlesnake! I mean, it's cool, but I don't dig it, don't get it! English here, please. I'm still learning, hun!"

Anyways, she's way too beautiful to be in hell with me. She tells some picking me off the street story. Sweet, but, I'm not buying. That I was not breathing, and, fearing I was some criminal, 'cause of the beard thing, she had some friend come and help her drag me up to her flat.

I mean, I still can't move. Not a broken back, but, feels like it. Not any broken bones, actually. She's some nurse at a hospital across from Notre Dame. Hotel God. Right! Or, Hotel Dieu the name?

I busted out laughing asking if I was kidnapped. Or, if I was being held for ransom. She says, "why would someone steal you?"

So, she has no idea who on earth I am? I mean, none! N-O-N-E! Now, that is a lie, impossible. Everyone knows me? Or, must know me?

Hell, is she the only person left on earth who doesn't know of me? I tell her my name's, Jim Morrison. The Doors and all. She says it means nothing to her. Only calls me, "James."

Only my mother called me James. And, my father when he was pissed. But, he just thought he ran my ass off, military style. Told her my father's the U.S. Navy Admiral. Told her they're all like that. Strict and unreasonable. Idiots!

Then, she fed me. She did not even seem to listen. Sour grapes, oranges. I passed on the bread and butter. Had the soft cheese. Goat milk?

13

Thought she had wine in the glass. She says, "no, no, no," and smiles. I want the wine! First time I see her smile. Really cute smile, too. Cuter face. Hotter body. I try to tell her I'm a rock star and that I've gone international. She laughs, says, "oui, me too, Monsieur James."

There's no phone here. I want to call Pam. Someone! I'll ask her to shave my beard. Itches like hell. Lice? When she comes back I'll ask for a razor!

I've lost all sense of time. Not a window in here to save my ass. See one in the other room, I think. Only two rooms in this castle's tower?

And, last night, I died then? Didn't feel it coming on. Can't believe it. Says she resurrected me? Mouth to mouth? Tender girl. What, all of 19? Saves Morrison's life? Great headline! Greater savior!

So, I slipped on through to the other side and didn't feel a god-damn thing? Damn! What a pity! Can't be! I missed it all?

Death is easy. Life's the bitch. I can't help but thinking and thinking about it. About, dying. About what she says must've happened last night. I try to remember but my head hurts when I do.

Through the locked doors this one comes to me? This young girl whose name I don't even know? And, where is Pam? Did she go to meet some trick, some dude in or out of Paris? This girl steals my heart. Pam's, lost it. This girl inspires me. Some kind of muse, Venus for sure. If only I could reach her. Touch her! She's so distant.

She touches my forehead, cheeks, not a fever. And, I want to grab her hand and kiss it.

I mean I always have taken what is mine. And, yet with her I can't just, 'go for it.' She's different that way. I must be in heaven. Or, no, just drunk.

Déjà vu?

I was humming my song. And, she heard it. Told her it was for her. She repeated after me, ever so slowly, so prettily, as I spoke,

"Slip, slip, slipping away.

I want you to take me away.
Love's forever we shall say.
Slip, slip, slipping away."

-------JDM

Her hands are soft, too. Pink. When she's here I want to stay. When I'm alone, I want to leave. "One day," she said, as to how long I've been here. Everyone will freak when I return. Dream's over. Another show tomorrow? Or, I'm a no show? I gotta go! Find my way back, re-invent some new Woodstock. This is crazy! I mean, she really saved my life? Then, it pisses me off. She cheated me out of it, outta hell. But, if it were not for her I'd want to die.

She's touched me in some way that I can't really say....

I'll kiss her on the lips, say, "merci!" Give her the 'au revoir' and split. I'll come back to Pam with a story. A song. Everyone will laugh, bitch me out. Fuck 'em! I mean we'll do the song and life'll go on. Always does. Hey, I'm on vacation anyways!

I'm ringing the bell she gave me, yell for her too! Oh, said her name's, 'Rose.' Rose! She'll come, I'll go.

"Slip, slip, slip away-----
out of this world, I'll take you away.
Here in my heart----
into my world you make me want to stay."

------JDM

I mean it's still unbelievable she don't even know of me. She lies! No, not her. But, how can it be possible? I'm more popular than god!

This obscurity she's lent me, I didn't even have in college. Everyone even knew me naked there! Not even in Florida, I suppose? I like it, liked it though. I long for my college days, again. Life was so easy....so easy being so unknown! Everything great ends too soon, even Sputnik after flying to close to the sun, fell.

She thinks I'm some criminal. I'll steal and hurt her heart, for sure. Not to do so is the crime. She makes me wonder. Pam only makes me think.

Rose makes me wish I could only go back in time when it was just me, alone. Obscure! Never thought of that until now, until her!

No one but me. No one. Myself. Me and I. Cause this is so luring. I'd rather be alone than lonely. Some glass ship sailing the seas, where anyone could see me, see through me but I'd be so far off into the sea no one would ever find me. But, I'd find myself, then. Be me, then.

Sun's bright rays and the bright blue of sky and sea would reflect my radiance eternally, out there…..

> *"Life's ship is just slipping away.*
> *I want you to be my ray of sun, eternally.*
> *Your ship slips, slips, slips away."*

----JDM

It's like I died and now I'm saved. I live, again. Then, I'm to go back into the world to die again? A very lonely death.

At the top of the mountain you can only see down. There's little breathing room up there. Little room for anyone. Easier to be a holy man on top of a mountain than among man.

They adorn me but they know not me. That drunken boat, me. That drunken captain, me. Just drifting. No land. Never any sight of land. No one. Nothing.

If it takes the blind to see, I want her to continue in her not knowing me. Then, she'll see the true and real me.

I must run! Let her, my fans, live vicariously through my fame. Throw them just the leftover morsels!

So, Rose, good-bye. Cause, I gotta go back. So much shit to do. Pam, too. Mile high agenda. Hey, it's been real! And, thanks for the song, Rose!

La vie en Rose!

-----JDM

DIARY ENTRY #2

Summer, July, 1971
Paris, France

"Slip, slip, slipping away....into the dark recesses so far away.
Here's where you only know my way,
slip, slip, slipping away....."

Can't write worth shit. I feel.....I don't know what I feel....why I feel what I feel. Don't think I feel much, not even anything. My soul numb. Even my toes tingle. My finger tips have no feeling and I shiver like ice.

Where am I? Don't know. Don't know what to say. Not even how to say it. Me, the master of words, the poet, the sage, speechless? Frightens even me to hell.

I don't remember much either. I know it had to have been some damn bar again, last night. Same story. Topless bars, little pills, big fat rolled ones, guzzling right from the 'ol bottle. Sounds familiar! My same shit life.

And, where the hell am I? This is not my apartment. This wall paper was not there. They moved me, again? I just want to write some poem, the next song they'll swallow up, and, I can't think....just spilling my guts, looking for a god, some god, any god. No way! What am I thinking? Such an opiate for the people is god!

Ah, so I am dead? Dying sure's the easy part of it all. Living is the real bitch. With that wall paper this is gotta be hell. Seems more appropriate than some heaven and harp shit, angelic voices and white flowing robes. Get me the fuck out of there!

Plus, more interesting people in hell I would suppose. And, so this is my season in hell? God shit? No god shit here! Only great illuminations! I have such great expectations!

So, I wake up in hell? So, then what was earth? God, my throat's on fire, burns.......hell, this is hell, then this makes sense. My head wobbles like waves. I want to, need to.....puke. I think I already did. God, I stink. I never thought that you could smell your own stink? Or, if you did you liked it? I hate it. Damn, red hot, my eyes burn too.

In a nice clean bed now, too clean though to be hell? I can't....no, not be in, no, this is hell. So, where the fuck is Rimbaud? My god. No? Not in heaven, he can't be.

Where is he then? Or, Nietzsche and Hendrix? God is dead? Who then's running this show then? I can't really move. My song book with me now, wet from some soaked street or rain. Damn!

I only remember taking a piss in that French toilet where two bars shared the same

pisser. Paris, the most incredible place on earth but why are the pissers here so fucked up? God, some damn hole in the ground. Some shit always here.

If only a word could come to me, some poem, some song. I need something new to dazzle them. Anyways, where's Rimbaud? This, my season in hell?

I lay on my damned fat belly, beard itches like lice swimming on my face! I can't hardly move. My hand writes and I just watch the pen move. No shit. Who the hell is writing this then? Not me.

Oh, shit!! I can't believe I did it. But, fuck them still! I just yelled, more like screamed, "RIMBAUD!" At the top of my lungs! Now, I hear some foot steps coming. Door must be locked, close to me though. My neck is so stiff. Hell, I could not write a song if my life depended on it. I am so disjointed. Is it Ray coming? Bernie? Then they must be dead too, if I am dead? So, why do I need a song then?

If there is a hell then there must be some god. And, I don't believe that shit. Never did. I hear some pump shoes, some chick walking. Some sexy broad? Send that blond bomb shell my way. Marilyn, that's you? Janice looking for a needle, flower in her hair? Mmmmm, smells good in here. I like hell, already!

Shit, I must be dreaming. I'm not that lucky to be dead. What if those girls are in heaven, that would mean....no, they're in hell. And, she did 'em all, used 'em all, did it all. I mean she is in hell with me, lucky me, sweet Monroe. So, when she comes in I'll see if she's been looking all along for, *Lord Jim.*

God, I ache. I wanted to die with my eyes open. Missed the whole damn thing.This little song,

"try and slip away, any way, with you...."
over and over, won't stop in my head.

------JDM

DIARY ENTRY #3

That damn crooked king sends us more and more, over and over, to the jungles to die. Like rats. It's not a war. It's a mass grave with no one wanting to fight 'cept the bankers, lawyers, Nixon and Khrushchev. As long as the fighting's not on our soil their concerns are met. Die, bleed, like rats on someone else's soil. Cold war, cold feet.

Hell, that is not fighting. That is not power. Power is having the ability to do something but not doing it. Our government can't get it? This is pure unadulterated killing. Period! A blood bath of the purest form and no one hears us.

When, when, when, when will it end? How long must we die for nothing? For some flag, some empty symbol they tell us means something. Brainwashing we have been told to die for. And, poor sons of bitches on both sides, die. It's barbaric. Treason of the soul. Man, give peace a chance!

They don't like Lennon, fear him, his songs, why they got him under surveillance. Mark my words, one day the heat will be too hot and the federal agents will have some patsy like Oswald take him out. Just like they did with JFK, RFK, Martin Luther King, Marilyn Monroe....the list goes on and on.

You know too much. You think too much. You say too much. You die!

Anyone who does not wake up with the flag in their bed gets buried with one on top of their coffin. Then, some lousy bugler plays taps. Noise. Stick that shit to the god-damn admirals! Yes, to my father, too! How long can we take it? One day maybe we the people will rise up? Let the revolutions begin! No more war! Peace to all brothers and sisters is not a dream! It can be a reality if we only give peace a chance. And, why can't we just give it a try? Damn if I know. Crooked kings, that's why.

Freud's right, man! It's all about our dicks, some fucking pissing contest out there with us being pissed on and us coming back in body bags! Their toys, their tanks, planes and bombs, the bigger the better. Show us how big your dick is when you use your bombs! Burn bras, then! Not people. I just can't take it anymore. Glad I left the US!

Every damn day on TV, radio, the newspapers, you see the names of the dead who are coming home. Everyday! It don't stop! I don't need any translation here. I know what it says. Same 'ol shit just another day.

Don't ever have to translate music, the language of the soul. Don't ever have to translate poems, the talk of the heart. This is 'cause from the cave we made music and poetry. The primal beast, beats.......bum, bum-bum, bum. Bum-bum, bum-bum, bum, bum. Like all music. Heart beat of mother earth. Like Elvis, or, when the Beatles were together, the Stones, Dylan. Bum, bum. Shit, The Doors! We touch 'em low and raise 'em high!

Here, in Paris, seems that's only what I hear! American music, rock and roll on the radio. It's cool! But, don't the French have their own music? I want to hear some torch song music, something French, something slinky, sexy, something by Edith Piaf. Kind of slutty! They only copy us.

But, man, Elvis is like a god here, bigger than god. And, I kind of like it that way. Religion's gods only let us down. Don't answer us, don't even listen. Our gods of music give us hope, inspire us, lift us up. Even share love, free love for all.

In our heaven we find a utopia filled without notice of sex, gay, bi, lesbian, color of skin, druggie, class or education. Come as you are. Party as you are! We'll do the rest. But, the government, religious powers don't want that. Gotta stop us. I'm glad that she, my Rose of roses, I call her, shut the god-damn radio off. My head pounds. With that beat. Bum, bum. Bum-bum.

I can hardly think, only wonder of the dead coming back home. From that so called war! They're all heroes, each one of them? Only hear of dead heroes, lately. So, get our guys home, alive if possible, just get us home! Don't they know that there are no winners in war? No one wins! 'Cept for the stock market kings, the wall street bankers, the crooked kings who fuel it all with green backs and oil. Man, how can they be so disgusting? People, wake up, rise up, get up from your asses and do something now! I swear, one day it will be too late!

Don't they see the red on their red, white and blue flag? The red is colored with blood. The red is on their green money, too. I can smell and even taste the blood from here. Shit, my head.

She gave me a phone. I called the states. Called some 'ol gals I used to call my sweeties. They all answered the phone calls. I'd hang up as soon as they would answer. They'd say, 'hello.' I'd think, yeah, it's her, and, I'd hang up. Telling Rose, no one's home. I only wanted to hear their voices, that's all. Just listen to them breathe. Them not knowing it's me. Funnier than shit! They'd hang up sometimes before I would. Why, I called at least a dozen or more. Some, I hadn't talked to since college, a few even from high school. Shit, quite a few years between us. And, I could still recognize their voices. Voices don't change much at all, even with age. Over the years they sound the same. I never knew that 'til today.

Some of their husbands would answer too. I'd say to them, 'fuck you' and hang up. Then, I'd know she tied the knot. I knew that she would never have been happy with me. One just never hung up the line, she just kept saying, "hello, hello, hello. Who is this? Who is this?" She should be so lucky if it was some rapist. I know she heard my Elvis playing in the background. *Hey baby, this is Jim. Remember me from a few years back?* As if I am gonna tell her it's me? Silly shit in their heads. They make me sick, too. I think too much, I think!

Think I can finally move my body a bit more today. Still sore. Feel paralyzed. I think that the 4th of July passed or is tomorrow, maybe yesterday? They got it here too, Bastille daze! Big drunken bash too, fireworks. Same shit! I just wanted to see the stars tonight. Some constellation. Maybe even mars, or, venus, or jupiter? Make pictures with the stars like you make pictures with clouds. Rose says it's too bright in Paris at night to ever see the stars. But, I just miss them. Tell her I see the stars in her eyes.

Rose helps me to a real live bathroom with a real seat in there, real shower too. Helps me shower, real toilet paper, too. Must be in heaven for sure with that!

Heard some chatting outside, down below the bathroom window. Hoped it was some lovers on some stroll. Wanted to yell, "hey, I'm Jim Morrison." Then, I don't, just want to hide from the world at the same time. Tomorrow, Rose says we go to my apartment in the Marais here in the city. Shit, I don't know where it is though. Not sure where I am at all. I don't remember much, much less know where I am. Don't know the phone number here or even there. Let them all think I've run off with some sexy babe. Fuck 'em! Tired of all this shit! I want to live. Want my life back, too!

Can't seem to keep much food down when I eat. She makes me some warm milk with slop or cereal in it. Hell, if I know. I started feeling better. When making the calls, I felt fine. Shit, I could have talked. They'd never have recognized this voice all burned out and hoarse. Seem I only feel empty inside. Feel lost, desolate. No one knows of my plight, the plight of a poet. No one knows this pain, no one will. The writings in this diary I will one day burn. But for now, it helps.

Books are like old friends, and, this song diary is a true friend to me these days. It's for my songs, poems, some lyrics, sketches and doodles. I put the book on my chest when I sleep so it rests on my heart. Hold it close. Imagine it's love. No one has ever loved me for me. I've never loved anyone for them, either, I suppose. Though, I've still loved everyone in some way or another, I think.

In California, the stars against the dark desert sky dance, I bet. I can envision them now,

> *"...gentle words ruled each night.*
> *Orbs sang.*
> *Your tender heart, danced.*
>
> *In the cosmos was the unspeakable silence.*
> *Only I could hear..."*

                                    JDM

I miss Pam, I suppose. She doesn't miss me. She's out lost in those stars somewhere! But, I miss Rose more whose only in the next room. She leaves my doors in here open now. This criminal she thinks I am...she maybe wants him to capture her heart? Take her soul as my prisoner? But, she promised me she is going to help me get to the apartment tomorrow. Says I should be up to it then, hopefully. By the Bastille it is, actually. We got to find it. Rose makes me dream,

"Beautiful forms danced before me, upon the light.
The eye beheld such beautiful a spirit.

And to where, I still wonder.
Love was me, was not you."

---------JDM

Rose calls me, "le voyou," means some rebel. Hell, I am the one and only, guilty as charged. Her clock chimes, one. Morning or night? I wonder? Or, day? I tell her let me take you to a Memphis road house. Hear some real delta blues. Or, some Alabama whiskey bar. Or, Turkey. Yeah, Istanbul, and smoke pot and run from the cops laughing, outsmarting the bastards. Or, Mexico, see the Maya temples. She just shakes her head, "no."

But, when I say Italy, oh, she raises her eyes! Rome. Florence. Let's have time slip away in Venice! I tempt her with, gondolas, vino in our hands, a bottomless glass.

Toasting life! She smiles but doesn't say a word, only keeps putting wet rags on my forehead. Only says Italia is her fantasy! I'll capture her, put it all into film I say! I mean I want to travel. Explore the world. Be some explorer but not just of emotions or of the heart, but of places too. My fantasy!

In my oedipal complex I want to rise up higher than life. Want to venture out into the stars. See life as brighter, brighter than any of the stars as I go out brighter than them all! Then, one day a new cosmos will be born. Want to go out on the town now. My favorite, Montparnasse awaits me. They all call me! Drinks on me!

There, at the, Moulin Rouge, Lautrec paints some delicious decadence without me. Damn! I want to go! Stop in at the Hotel Alcance where Oscar Wilde died. I loved that hotel...now, I know they killed Wilde too, because he was gay, a 19th century hippie.

Our greatest visionaries of world's past they kill. They jailed him, set him free to die. Maybe one day they'll kill Elvis? Say it's some heart attack or drug overdose?

Want to go to the Beaux Arts and drink coffee with Picasso, Camus, Gide and Sartre. Over by the St. Germain church, there. Charlemagne came there 1000 years ago. The Devil's god. Want to drink coffee at Deux Magots with the greats. Never see them talk philosophy that much anymore. Is Camus dead? I think…..yes.

Want to join in sometime. Tell them my philosophy. Shout it out! Scream my ideas my feelings as loud as I can from the tables. I speak for us all, I'll tell them! And, maybe they'll just listen to us! To their electric shaman. My words echoing in space!

We got to exorcise these demons which are only our fears of sex, I'll tell 'em! So, stick these leather pants and lizard kings and dark angels up your asses! I just want to be heard! Taken seriously, too! Want to be a writer, some great poet. Someday they'll listen to me! I only want some respect!

My exile, my night away from it all, and I'm here in this place I'm not even sure exists. Maybe this time someone will listen?

-----JDM

DIARY ENTRY #4

God-damn! This night is so damn dark. Inside I feel so sad, so alone. Abandoned.

My eyes must be cut inside. Bleeding. The pain lingers on, still hurting so badly. I cry. I know I won't sleep now. Can't. I sleep all day. But, I'm so tired all night. Must sleep. Hear Rose sleeping. But, in the next room.

I feel as if my life is on a downward spiral. I wish she was up so we could speak of life all again. But, why should I bring her life down, too? She has a whole life to live and be happy with. I am only her burden. I wish not to curse her life, but, I do feel something for her. Something I have never felt before. I am the albatross around her neck. The one which flies onto Baudelaire's ship and is stranded. Unable to fly, then, is killed by the barbaric crewmen. Am I that bird to her? Or, one of the crewmen?

I keep thinking that my life will only be the ruin of hers. I only became a singer due to never having my poems published, or, taken seriously. Then, the poems were published and my world changed. I thought if I sang some songs I could share some poems. And, if I was famous that my poems would be recognized, too. Taken seriously. Feel that no one refers to me as a poet. Like they do, Dylan. Then, when I finally had them published no one says a word! What do I write for then? To many, I'm just the fool on the hill!

If I died would the fact that I was a poet ever be printed in my obituary? I suppose I could now find out. But, it seems that so many bad poets exist! And, when I'm dead will the world think I was another bad poet?

I just hate it when some critic refers to me as, an aspiring poet. I have written a thousand poems. Some, published. Many not. So, I am NOT aspiring. Unheard, unrecognized for my real gift, yes! But, I am NOT aspiring. I wish it could be said that I was or am a poet. That's all.

There is a difference between a good poet and a bad poet. A great poet has long periods of time when they can't write. Can't think. Can't do anything. But, a bad poet writes and writes and writes. They never have writer's block. I have it always.

But, tonight I was inspired to write this. It is dedicated to Rose. Afterall, she is the one who saved my life. My Rose,

"The wish to sleep, mine.
To enjoy those moments of peace, my dream.

Not in life, though, do I find such a dream.
Only in death must we perish desires?

Oh, repose, sing unto me.
Sing the praise of sleep, of rest.

For never have I found a lullaby of solace.
Oh, restful night, forever must I remain against these
warm Paris nights as restless?"

-------JDM

Why must there be so much frustration when someone can't sleep? When insomnia comes? Nothing here to smoke or drink, either! How can there be so much irritation when one tries to sleep and can't? This is when one wishes to die. For then there's rest.

And, I feel it now..........with the back drop being the night itself.

---------JDM

DIARY ENTRY #5

The assassins have triumphed! They have finally killed me as well. What have they done to their son? To kill the demon you kill the god? Kill the angel at the same time? They've rebelled for the last time against the quintessential rebel! Exorcised the demon which was also once their demon. A dramatic death is a tragedy in the theatre of life.

"Mesmerize.
Anesthetize me.
Eulogize man!
Not one shall leave alive.

Souls die.
Hearts close under coffin's lid..."

------JDM

Now, it is clear. No memory block. My flat, 17 Rue Beautreillis, Paris, France. The river Seine nearby. Close to the Café de Flore where I'd written so many poems over the past months. Been here in Paris for 5 months, to escape, to be a writer! I had forgotten the address but as we walked, I spotted it. Here, I had fled to Paris, been exiled here to finally come to life. As well as meet my death. The dark angel dies as all angels weep!

God-Damn!

A god-damn coffin comes out from the behind the doors. A hearse stands guard. I finally see Pamela, some record reps, some fans, a doctor, I suppose, and police. Pamela doesn't look too upset! Some wife! From a distance I hide, stand under a canopy and just watch. Now, I'm Mr. Mo Jo Risin.' A bandana of red over my head, standing hunched over on crutches and no one recognizes me. Rose accompanies me. And, soon, she walks up to them, speaks to them, asks them something. They tell her Jim Morrison died in a bath tub. Heart attack brought on by drugs, pills and booze. Some cop's speaking to her.

I see Pam touch the wooden casket. I want to walk towards her, but as Rose returns, she becomes frantic, saying, "it can't be that way." She wants to walk away from it all with me.

She begins showing me that a bright star's light has been extinguished. The bright star, Morrison!

She whispers in my ear, "but, another cosmos can now be born, James." I break into tears, asking, "but, whose inside the pine box? Pamela set this up?"

Thought that Pam was sipping wine in Bordeaux. I still don't get it. It seemed to rain harder and harder as I slipped a few times on the wooden tips of the crutches.

We hobbled from canopy to canopy, stairway to stairway, to stay dry. Dogs seemed to be everywhere. I stepped in shit over and over. Never noticed this before. Wet shit makes me almost fall, again! So damn slippery is shit! Rose keeps holding me by the side. It's like a movie when you see your own death flash before your eyes.

Back here at Rose's, I long for drink, a smoke. I plead. She gives me a glass. I take the bottle.

Pam did know my wish to slip away, disappear, return to obscurity. But, man, holy shit! Rose says it's an empty box. But, Pam looked too calm, too reserved. I think I remember Pam's eyes meeting mine, her recognizing me for a split second. Rose says we were not that close, not possible. Pam was carrying the type-writer, my papers.

I long for hash, some weed, some peyote. I want to invoke my ancestors in the names of, Sitting Bull, Geronimo, Cochise. To smoke the pipe with them seeing the buffaloes and mountains hovering above the plains. Tell them that their descendants also have visions and are filled with wonder. What have they done to their son?

Rose says it's on the radio, American rock and roll legend, James Douglas Morrison dead at the age of 27. *Apparent drug over-dose in a Paris bath tub. Perhaps a heart attack, no autopsy scheduled.* What is all this shit with bath tubs? I haven't been in a bath for weeks, god damn! I have a hell of a lot better taste than to die naked, shit faced in some slum lord's apartment in a god damn bath tub! Shit!

Rose puts her arms around me. Says when one star novas another cosmos is create. I've heard it all before. She calls me her star. But, what of Pamela? I'll never see her, never be with her again? Ever? I treat her badly, she loves me madly! And, so this is Pam's final gift of love to me? To set me free?

Says on the radio I'm to be laid to rest at Pere Lachaise cemetery here in Paris. Hell, I was just there! What, two, three days ago? Put me near Chopin, or, Wilde!

Rose said that today my face looked different, relieved, unburdened. Not so pale, my face not so fat. I don't know. Must be from losing the beard?

They keep playing, *Light my Fire*, some tribute to me on the radio. Rose comes in as I scream to her, "we gotta go to Pere Lachaise!" She says it is not possible. That I will be found out. Maybe I want to be found out? Maybe I want my old life back? I do want it back, I tell her!

She says, "no, no, no, James, been a long day. Get some rest my dear."

"No shit! I am going to be buried," I yell back at her!

When I'm to buried, I want some satyrs in my funeral procession, want Bacchus playing the flute and marching down the Champs Elysees announcing, *"Jimmy's got the whole world again! That which was dead, is now alive! Jim's been risen from the dead!"*

I want to hear at the funeral that Dionysus has given me my life back through some perverted ritual called, *death*. And, now, this rock star can dream again of far away places where no one knows his name, his face. Where he will know no one.

I only want to be able to wake to music which does not sound so damn western. Music I've never heard of, can't figure out. I want to hear someone speaking in a language where I don't recognize a word in their sentences. I mean something different! A place, a culture, unknown even to me. Where all the customs are unique to me.

Where say, shaking hands with someone means you sentence them to death. Insult them. I want something new, different!

I want to wear the garb of indigenous peoples. Never wear pants or shirts and shoes again! Wear some robes, some toga, some towel, hell if I know. I want to exit this civilization. Escape it for good. Maybe Africa? Asia? Find a new path to follow.

Say, sell coffee, run guns, slaves, like Rimbaud. Go where no white man's ever been. Where they will stare back at my stares at them. And, women will giggle and point at me behind veils of ignorance. Where I can live life again, and where I can lead a band and no one will order me what to sing. Some place where I can write all night and sleep all day. Play my guitar, beat a drum, whistle, or, play some instrument I never knew existed before.

Forget about the music and lyrics which have been ruined by the greed and lies of capitalism. Of commercialism. Where I can sing my poems. Make my own beer, my own wines, grow poppies, watch deserts completely change before my eyes as sands blow here, then there. Feel what thirst is like again, what hunger feels like. Never need electric again, or, air-conditioning. Seasons will not be hidden from the power of the earth ever. I won't be insulated from something so powerful as nature! I want to dance! I can dance naked there all night long before a fire, making music in beats and tones no man's ever known before.

So, now I am a man who rises from the dead celebrating my divinity. Not even Christ was so powerful, so lucky! Some phoenix from the ashes. I want to gaze upon the pyramids, seeing Giza and knowing my own afterlife is now, invoking Osiris's name and living yet another day!

I want to belong, I tell Rose. I've been re-created. I want to belong! To live, create a brotherhood of man, of women, where sisters walk hand in hand with brothers. Where black embraces white, and, white embraces black. Where east meets west and Vietnamese meet Americans and smile, embrace each other in a silent sense of peace. Or, am I only dreaming?

I can begin my life anew, my wish has come true. I am not dad. I am very much alive! I rose above my humanity, grasped at truth and felt death's hand walk me towards life. I mean how totally cool!

Some are born to lead, some to follow. I was born for music. To create it, yes, to hear it sure, but born to feel it, more. So, I wait, wonder and listen, hearing only the voice still speaking, laughing, reminding all, '*you too are next.*' Knowing that this time I cheated the grim reaper.

I accept that like the flower I shall again fade, but, just next time not from glory.

Finally, I've broken on through to the other side.

-------JDM

DIARY ENTRY #6

I wish I could play the harp. Then she could hear what my soul sounds like as I long for her this night. This dark night of the soul.

I've invaded her bookshelves here. I've developed my voracious appetite again for books. I read and read, reading the erotic poems of St. John of the Cross. Who needs the Marquis de Sade when you can hear the lustful passion to a god through a saint?

The dark night of his soul, a love poem to a lover. Some say it's to god. Some say it is to some other. Don't mention the unspeakable name of the illusion of John's lust. A night like mine too, now filled with loneliness and despair, delusion. I still can't begin to phantom that which I saw today. What I felt. A wooden casket......

I've read his poem over and over while listening to some Japanese music, so peaceful, so respite. Short-wave radio would make someone a god today, say, in the Amazon. Let it be me!

The music of harps resonate so deeply within my soul, lingers within me throughout the night. The dark night of the soul, my face upon my lover's breast. It is so clear that this John was passionately in love with the man Jesus, the one he called his god. But, this saint was able to be passionate without his god, as I am so passionate without her love, even without Pam near me now. Miss Rose, more.

Damn!

Wanted a poem!

My writing seemed to be flowing out from me so much tonight. My words, gone. Now, seems like a fog inside my brain. I had felt inspired.

Now, I just don't want the muse's touch to abandon me, leave me alone this night. This night, especially. For the touch of the muse was there. Will it finally return? Or, is it gone like the wind?

I remember an Irish poet's words, "*the world is filled with more weeping than one understands.*" Yates? I understand it now, fully understand it in this very moment. I can hear in between Rose's breathing a very soft rain falling. So pretty, so lovely. It falls amidst the summer flowers in the French capital. It's magnificent. Makes everything so alive, so wondrous a color of green, deep and elusive.

And, so, within all this beauty my heart turns towards her. All I have, left. Towards nature's Rose.

--------JDM

DIARY ENTRY #7

Shit man! Woke in a fucking panic! Screaming! My heart beating faster than hell! Covered in a sweat. Wish I had a handful of painkillers and a bottle to wash them down with. Damn, I don't remember falling asleep either. I tell Rose everything's great. But, these mothers of nightmares again! Will they ever stop? Know thyself?

Some snake trying to kill me. Though I've never been afraid of them, not even poisonous ones, but this one freaks me out. This one in my nightmare was one I had as a kid. But, I thought it was a beautiful snake, *Sheba*, but, I dare not get so close to her. Black and smooth, like freshly tanned leather.

Well, then in the dream she turns on me. Becomes mean and ugly, poisonous too. But, I keep remembering how she was once calm and gentle. She would even sleep on my chest. In my dream she has fangs, was trying to bite me, kill me. So, I had to kill her first and I knew I would. I killed her in the dream. It was a lot just to capture her. And, even in the dream what was so difficult for me was that I knew in my heart just how gentle she really was. But, I was still driven, compelled by some primal instinct to kill her.

Have I lost control? To thy own self be true?

She was stalking me, setting me up for the kill. I had to do it. Just had to.

Maybe driven like a man who has a rabid pet he must shoot? Or, a horse one loves having a broken leg and you have to put it down? It must be done. Heart battling it out with the mind. Mind dueling with the heart. The mind says, "do it." The heart says, "no, never." It was nearly impossible to choose but my mind won out in the end. Not sure if I am

35

happy with the outcome. But, I knew it was needed to be done to save me.

Do or die. Kill or be killed. I still regret the action. It feels like I really did kill her.

Rose says that she read that Freud said the snake symbolizes sex. Like in the Bible story of Adam and Eve. The lure of sex over man? Why have we come to believe that sex is evil? "Nothing new," says Rose, "4000 year old fear." So, it's really about power. The same with the garden of good and evil. It symbolizes man's sexual nature. The serpent tempts this Eve into eating a dumb ass apple. Then they both see each other's nakedness, their SIN! Now, to get rid of the sin they need the god to become clean again. Very clever! About power, the opiate or control over the people.

Simple and clear to only me? But, I am still unclear what this nightmare meant in relation to my life? Can dreams have universal meanings like Freud said? I think that a dream only means what you decide it means to you. Dream on!

Now, I'm afraid as hell to fall back asleep. But, I keep thinking just how my dream relates to my life and what my inner dream world is trying to tell me. I can't help but think how all my thoughts, my poems, come from my unconscious, from past ancestors, recent relatives. ALL the minds of those who lived prior to me. Maybe even past lives? Some people just seem too enlightened to have only lived once.

Maybe my dream of me killing the snake means I won the revolt against the chains of society? 'Cause I've read about synchronicity and the collective unconsciousness. I think I am right. That makes sense. Rose thinks so, too.

Maybe my poems or my thoughts are not even my own? Only influenced by the dreams and demons of the past? Of past peoples, past generations upon me? Hmm, Jung seems to think so, Rose says. I think so too! It's gotta be…

I'm' very lucky to have been born a singer and a poet. Seems some folks are either one or the other. I'll try to write more hoping that these voices inside me come out and help me. I'll rely on my past. The past loves, those whose names and voices are nameless, unknown. Those who crawled from out of the mud, those who walked through sands and forests. Fought to be civilized. Loved me, but, left me lonely. But, there's still too much mud left on humanity's feet these days.

With my pen in hand I'll write, I swear. I'll let their voices guide me this dark night of the soul. Let them channel their words through me hoping that in their seductive séance through me, I'll set their story, man's story straight.

-----JDM

DIARY ENTRY #8

Hell, yea! I've been born again! Yee haw!!! Mr. Mo Jo Risin's been reborn! Take that you ignorant preachers! How is that dear father, my old priest! Raising hell, here! Yeah!

We soared down the Boulevard de Menilmontant in some long cylindrical tube, kind of phallic looking too. Fast, delirious. Right past the gates where you enter the cemetery. One hell of a bus ride.

The cemetery. Towering, mighty walls! Looking up! Thick, iron gates! Protecting the dead? A fortress for what? Why lock up the place? What if someone wants to stroll in a graveyard at night contemplating their own existence?

Don't these guards have those feelings too? Were they trying to keep the dead in? Or, the living out? Fucking beats me! Royal A-1 assholes, the superficial who never suffer from an existential crisis. Deep, deep, bastards!

Just like the high school punks who become cops! Those who join the military! Bullies for hire!

Got some coffee at some dive of a coffee house with the Church of the Madeline staring at us from across the street. Don't remember getting off the bus, though. I found some little red pills which rolled out on the floor from my jeans. Swallowed them up fast. Looking out the window seeing her reflection in the window, Rose and I sipped coffee. It was really dark out. I was kind of shaking. Light rain and a speedy buzz. But, I insisted that this was the night to go to Pere Lachaise. I smoked, nervously awaiting the right time to go in.

As we drank, it seemed like lights zoomed on by like on the bus. Traffic died down, it was finally time. She knew a place right off the boulevard where we could get in, where the bars on the rawd iron fence swung like some guillotine's blade. Back and forth, up and down too. Easy as hell!

I needed to know so I kept asking Rose, "is the dirt in the graveyard sand? Or, clay? Or plain old mud?" Why was she so pissed? I couldn't remember much. Some guards in there, watch dogs too. Holy shit! The police scared her, she was real uptight. I told her it was all bullshit lies. We are only with ancient spirits, at peace with them in there. How'd she know of this broken fence then? She gave me the evil eye! Still pissed.

Would there be many flowers? The grave shallow? Not some damn cross on my grave?

I felt dizzy, confused. I held my little book of poems. A new one from her. I always carried the works of Rimbaud with me. It was even with me when she found me. I kept thinking of his line, my line too, "I'm interested in anything about revolt, disorder, and, chaos." Hey, that is exactly like me!

Over and over I thought Rimbaud was me. Me, him. I was his reincarnation! I told this all to Rose, thinking aloud. But, then she yelled, "please stop! I can't believe I am doing this, let's go, Jim!" First time she ever called me Jim? Was that a good or a bad sign?

Finally got in! "I'm a Roman Catholic, just ask Mother Church!," I tried to tell her. "And, it's a Catholic cemetery! Rose, the Mother Church has one hell of an Oedipal complex!" The evil eye comes again aimed right at me.

Hell, it's my grave, I can go anytime I want, right? She's not laughing!

The bars were really rusty, cut my hands. Squeaking for oil. Barely could squeeze my body in. Walked on pebbles crushing under foot. Good thing all my clothes were black and camouflaged against the night. She looked for my grave's section, lighting a match, looking at some paper. We walked and walked.

Lost.

She saw a site with several burning candles. Wasn't mine. Cats prowling everywhere! Smelling like piss everywhere! She knew the place just not in such darkness, utter fog. I made some ghoulish sounds and she hit me! For hours we kept looking.

"On the road with Jack Kerouac," I began to say, as we marched on, then, I felt it, "stop! Here! This is it! I think," I screamed, "HOLY SHIT!" More flowers and candles than Cleopatra would believe. TONS! All for me! Rose could not believe them all. There were piles, mounds of them! She sat nearby on an old tomb, tired, resting and fatigued.

Then, all of a sudden, just like a bat out of hell, pushing flowers aside, I began to dig.

She grabbed me, saying, "no!" Me pushing her aside with great force. I had to do this. I felt compelled. I had no choice. She tried to push me off the grave. But, I dug like some damned mad dog with my cupped paws. My hands got numb fast, bloody from the sand's crystal razors. A very shallow grave for sure!

She began to cry and stomped away, leaving me all alone. "Hit the road," I roared!

I dug out sand like making some sand castle on the beach. I kept digging. Would there be a cross inside it? Some smelly corpse rotting for the last two weeks? I felt the top of the box!

I pulled one end of it up a bit and tried to rip off the top. The whole top should've opened but since the back of it was in the dirt the top of the casket would only open a bit. I began to shake more, shiver, it was cold down there. My blood mixing in the sand. Finally, it opened! Empty bottles of cheap wine and open cigarette packs fell in on me.

I pushed the box to the side of the open grave. As it opened without a noise, not even a squeak, I lit a match. Needed a cigarette! Lit one! I heard a voice! The crumbling of the stone's path. Some cops? Rose? Two voices. Holy Mother of God! My heart was beating so fast thought I'd die of some heart attack for real this time. Die in my own grave. They'd find me dead with the stupid assed French suspecting someone tried to dig me up. Fucking French, they'd just rebury me. Shit!

The voices came nearer, closer. I put out my smoke. I heard, "think it's over there!"

"No, here, somewhere." Voices began to fade. Me, so relieved. She said to him that she wanted to conceive their baby on my grave! Make love with Jim below us! Fuck 'em! I had become an aphrodisiac?

Finally, I lifted the long lid and glanced inside. No more matches left. I knew it. Had to be. There it was! A bag of leather. Some black purse. Soft, heavy, full. I unzipped it. Smelled it, wads of cash, yes! "Oh, Pam," I kissed the bag. Just knew it! Tossed the bag up.

From my pocket placed the book of Rimbaud poems, inside. Gently sealed the lid. Didn't see a soul or a body in my casket. Good, I'll need it one day!

Began to throw the sandy dirt over the empty box, kicking more in with my feet into the grave. I was soaked in sweat! My eyes burned from the salty sweat pouring into my eyes. Sweat, rain, over-heated. Kind of freaked. Put some of the dead flowers on the top of the covered grave. Finally, it was covered!

Grabbed for the bag. But, couldn't find it. NO FUCKING WAY!!! The candles were out. Where was the bag? Couldn't see shit. I walked and looked around, slower each time. Got on my belly moving my feet and arms like an angel looking to touch the bag. Nothing! That bags my life! Was it accidentally buried again below? Just fell in? Where the fuck was Rose? I was so exhausted, ready to die, so thirsty! The bag was not near any of the other tomb stones or mausoleums or graves. I wanted to cry in utter frustration! Just wanted to die.

And, where was the tomb stone for my grave? Just some wooden stick there? What kind of shit was that?

Then, I heard another voice. Whispering, "looking for this?" Who said that? Rose threw it at me, "here, I could kill you!" I pled for us to go, she said, "it's now or never!"

We walked away without shoes or socks. She said someone's in here. She had her shoes in her hand. Where were mine? I said I heard them too. Had glass in my toes, stones buried deep in my feet. Shhhhh! We heard them. FUCKING! They think that that's my grave over there! Dumb fucks! They weren't even on my grave, idiots!

And, conceiving their child on my grave, their aim, was it some ritualistic ecstasy? Bastards! We giggled as I made a loud fart noise. A real stinker under the arm! There was silence, then, their pumping began again! More farts. Think they ran off?

We walked for a while but knew we were lost! The sky was getting lighter and lighter. We made it, finally, the fence. Couldn't go on though. So tired, so beat! We had to get out soon! But, when we checked, none of the bars of the fence moved. We ran down further and further pushing on the bars. Nothing. Frantic!

We ran down more and more trying to get a bar to move. Not a one. We sat against a grave stone. Sat down, finally! Bag on my lap, her hand on mine, my head on her shoulder.

We woke at what seemed like noon. Hot sun, blistering humid summer heat. She had just put on her shoes when she screamed. Some cat was eating a dead bird! A bad omen she said. I rolled my eyes when I saw it. "Kiss me Rose, kiss me!" She hesitated and I took her neck with my hand pulling her head towards mine, her lips touching mine. "Kiss me," I whispered.

Enthralled, our eyes closed, we heard a whistle blow. Then a cop came running over. Not a real cop, no gun! She kept on kissing me, though. The cop rattling off some French shit! "Shut the fuck up," I said to him! "Fuck? Fuck?" Him knowing what it meant! She explained something keeping her hand over my mouth! My tongue licking her palm. The cop accused us of coming in only to hide and kiss. Rose told me he told us to get a room for that! I'd told him to fuck off.

Then, several guards and some with dogs huddled around us. They didn't patrol all night, only began at dawn, lazy lying asses. She laughed when we walked out through the gate's bars, singing, "just like in the movies!"

In the bag, money. Money. Money! And, a letter. On the envelope, JIM. From Pam? "Had to be," Rose said. But, Rose also said that I stunk! Finally home. My bath was to be now. Soon, we were to eat! She said something about me still being ill. Our first shared meal!

Candles burning already. She took the letter from my hand pointing to the bath tub. My feet like I was in a sand box. I was relieved to be back here, kind of felt like my home. I quickly going mad over what Pam's letter will say…..

------JDM

DIARY ENTRY #9

A new archetype of man has been born! One who wants to experience a new consciousness, a new way of seeing the world where a new vision transcends all thought. Doubt, is suppressed. Our destiny is clear. A metamorphosis only those in a new age could understand.

I sat. Smoked. Drank. Pondered it all. Stared at the blank desk. I was an anxious to open the letter, rip it open, but, too nervous to. Was it good-bye? Farewell, forever? Or, some rendezvous time and place? Then, what of Rose?

That little red headed Pam married me. Buried me. Gave me back my life even if I didn't like her folk music shit. This money would now finance my journey's march with Alexander's zeal alongside me as, *James the Great.*

But, what would it say? This letter of Pam's. I was so afraid to open it. I never feared anything like this before. Never encountered anything like this before…

Rose says I've been here well over two months now. How? Can't be. Why is Rose lying to me? Can't sleep. Want some sleeping pills, sleep for a year would be my dream.

Some radio news fiend says that now I belong to the ages, that now I'll be 27 eternally. I feel like 97, though. How many more rumors will go on of me dying? Reports of me still alive, still dying. Even sightings of me. I've heard dozens of rumors of my death over the years. No one is buying this one, 'cept for those who've wanted to do me in. They cheer. Kill somebody famous and you go from nobody to world famous

in seconds. Death threats at a dime apiece would've made me rich since the start. Wishful thinking.

Since I won't read the letter now, I've tried thinking of a poem or two to write. But nothing flows. Writing can be a curse. A place where I become trapped in a world of discomfort and pain. Pain was made to guide us to our humanity, grow and learn from. Pain is not negative if we use it wisely. But, it hurts wildly. I can't escape my senses. Try to but it doesn't work for long. It's a curse this life of a poet, writer, musician, artist. Anyone with a creative spirit knows this plight of emptiness, this eternal damnation.

Pain opens your eyes but still, crushes your heart. I can't sleep. Can't stay awake. Feel the need to write but the voice inside my head keeps commanding me, ordering me to write. *You are useless if you do nothing*, I hear inside me. Yet, I can't.

Such emotional turmoil deep inside my soul.

My toast to the night, is this,

Mirror the reflection beneath,
as you bequeath your radiance in shine of an afterglow.

For to mystify...
Stupefy...
Sometimes ratify a way...

Is magnificently your way,
glass of wine in bottled time.

-----JDM

DIARY ENTRY #10

9, September, 1971
Paris, France, 924pm

Earlier today I was sitting on the steps of some church, I think. Some old fuck had a monkey and a music box. Wanted a fucking dime. Get away from me you little freak! Threw the coin at the pet. It jumped and screeched! I watched them scurry away laughing my ass off at the pathetic sight.

I realized then that these pages have become a diary of sorts to me, really. Don't remember when they were writ, these entries. Much less remember even writing some. I had a diary before. When I was a kid. Put a lot of my songs in it, too.

So, how do I proceed with this diary? Must I date each entry even if I don't feel like it, or forget to? Do I begin with, '*dear diary*,' now? Shit, that would be sick!

I mean I never had time to write about me or life before. The great poets did. Say, Blake. I want to read his poems but I want to know of his life. I suppose you learn a lot from their diaries. Blake smoked opium which really is cool. So, with a diary your life has to be on display? Fuck that! No way with me.! No one will see this shit. I will burn all this in Mexico at some Maya pyramid one day! A tribute to the gods, goddesses, witch doctors, healers who've walked on this plain of earth with me.

Lately, I seem to care less and less of a revolution of many. I only want a revolution of one. Of me. I seem so powerless over myself. If the others will rise up, I can't know, nor care. But, we all must rise up against ourselves. Crush the inner beast inside each of us, never let it crush us. Ah, kind of like my snake dream! That 'blond beast' prowls and lurks in each one of us, says Nietzsche.

We must tame it, harness it or it will rage out of control ultimately destroying us. We're essentially still animals and its probably next to impossible to subvert our own evolution.

Where I sat at a cozy coffee shop today in Republic Square, near our flat, I watched that antique ferris wheel go round and round. Some lit up carousel, I wished it would spin off rolling down the street giving those plebeians inside one hell of a fucking ride. Wake their tamed asses up!

No one ever recognizes me anymore, like when I was with Pam. No one ever talks to me. I kind of like it but it's kind of lonely, too.

Clean shaven, baby round face, very short hair. Look 17 more than 27. Cotton shirts, bright and white. Cotton pants, brown and loose. Bohemian drifter, the look.

At times, with the loss of notoriety, I feel like I really did die. That some part of me actually did die, that I'm really not quite whole. I wonder if I am even happy now. I know happiness is not objective or universal. It's up to us to direct our own happiness, create our own destiny. But, how when you are so damn worn out? Can hardly get out of bed.

To me, *living is meaning.* If I look for meaning outside myself I'm immediately lost in the abyss, frightened and searching. Falling into a deep void I'll never climb out of. Some existential crisis. That's why I want Rose to go with me to the, '*Eternal City*,' Rome. There'll I'll find some meaning, some purpose to my life. When I look at her, her supple skin, warm brown eyes, I want to love her.

And, Pam haunts me, but she knows like me, that love is not exclusive to one person. You can love many people. Love can be for life, a year, a night. Even in a glance one can find an eternity of love in another's eyes. Whoever says *no* is not living. Some lovesick fool. We fall in love many times everyday, many times. Woman who poured my thick coffee today, I loved her in a moment's glance. And, I believe she loved me in return.

Rose and I dine each night, together. Rose sets the table like a Cézanne painting, in his honor. She comes from work, eats, sleeps, goes to bed only to do it all over again. Why is she reduced to some automaton? Some robot? What kind of shit is that for a life? Sisyphus had a better fate. After dinner, we always walk along the river in Republic Square. Looking at the boats going into the tunnel. She laughs when I tell her, *'that boat will never be seen again, ever.'* Disappears, transformed into a crystal ship. Now, transparent and unseen for eternity!

Here, nights are cool. Never knew that before, so, the sweaters don't' keep us that warm. We huddle closer in the chill, stroll down the avenue, walking and walking.

Sometimes we wind up at the Place de la Concorde. Looking over the traffic at the Champ Elysees. We sit and watch people. Stare at the Arch of Triumph. I tell Rose that I built it for her. We watch a building, the Louvre, marveling. Then, I always try to climb the obelisk brought back from Egypt in the middle of the square. She places her hands over her eyes, peaking......really loving it. We walk across the Pont Alexander, our romantic bridge, as I point towards the mint telling her that this is where I spend my days...printing money.

We listen to the city sounds, smell the city air. Gaze in wonder at the Eiffel tower which seems like some star following us everywhere we go. Look up, it's there. Other day a plane flew under the tower, French cops running after it, freaking. Me, laughing my ass off. Go rebel, go!

By day I read, write, wander, me exploring the city. Found the very first Paris, ever! And, by mistake! At the end of the square of Notre Dame you go down some steps and you're below the street on an island which was once Paris. They call it, "*Lutetia*."

There, they've even excavated Julius Cesar's campfire when he came here to Gaul.

I laugh at the tourists buying balloons, watching jugglers pickpocket them, cheating them out of money on postcards, silly shit souvenirs. They've not found Paris. I want to share this with Rose. Show her the Paris I've found. Visit where Hemingway and Jefferson dined, in the restaurant, *Procop*. But, I would only go there and sign their guest book, like they all did, with someone I love. Regret never taking Pam.

In my new neighborhood, I'm seen as a French intellectual. Maybe some professor at the Sorbonne even, with my beret and long stoic face.

I've been learning how to speak a little French. Know how to say, 'fuck you,' and, 'asshole.' But, now, I need to, I want to get away. But, I can't leave her.

Went to the cinema alone, today. They're all crazy over, '*The French Connection*' and, '*Love Story.*' Oh, saw this movie, '*Harold and Maude.*' Very neat ideas on funerals, death, love. Dark and maybe morbid, but, funny as hell. Made me think.

Oh, got a pocket radio. I listen to music a lot. Even my own! I think, rest, even cook, these days. I've told Rose I want a life with her. Let's go, *mon cher amour*. She rolls her eyes, only smiles. With or without her I'm soon to go. Leave Paris, I tell her. To find a life, any life, find myself, find love. Why can't it be with her? Why won't she simply just say, 'oui?' I feel locked out of the world. A prisoner. Rather be dead if I can't escape soon.

But, will she follow? I am afraid, not.

-----JDM

DIARY ENTRY #11

The best of times. The worst of times.

With her I again stood in the Place de la Concorde. Stood in the same exact spot where the guillotine hovered high above heads. A shiny blade and soft drum rolls turned the street's gutters red. Flowing with blood.

Kings. Nobles. Marie Antoinette.

Revolutions are great, but always bloody if worth their salt.

My memory returns to that place. Where the eternity of darkness began for so many. Lifting heads out of baskets showing them to onlookers, cheering, jeers.

One can't help but reminisce. Think, *nostalogize.* Is that a word? I'll always return to my Helen within Paris; here at our rock of Troy.

------JDM

DIARY ENTRY #12

1st, November 1971
All Saints Day. 33. Rainy in Paris

Jim-------

If you're reading this now, you got in and got the bag and figured it
out. I know it's crazy but it's worked so far. Keep out of the spotlight,
keep a lid on it. It's hard for me to say, but, if you love something set
it free. If its yours it comes back. If it don't it wasn't meant to be.
Some poet said this, Jim, maybe even you? I know I didn't say it as
good as you. But, what it means is I am setting you free. I want you to
have the life you've talked of for so long. I don't want to see you go
down with those charges. Or, hear critics be cruel to you and the
music. Or hear Nixon cheer some Nazi groupies burning your music.
How else could've I set you free if I did not give you something to
spend? We have to keep it cool for a bit. But, when the time is right
we will catch up again. Don't worry. We will.

Watch for my sign!

I promise I won't ever stop loving you.

--------Pam

Lead this cold, lonely existence here. Not Pam, not Rose. All Saint's
Day. Remember it back in Pensacola when we went to our catholic
church. Know of St. James.

51

Woman at the bakery, Madame Dufray, says, '*in the air you can feel the cold of the dead.*' Tomorrow, All Soul's Day. All Parisians on holiday. The city to be empty and quiet. Icy today too, summer's gone. Like it like this. All to myself in Paris.

So gray and brown, depressing. All I see is a death of the city here. I walk, talk, stalk my next destination to write with this as my backdrop. I've written what seems like hundreds of songs as of late. Write them, then, throw them away. Mean nothing to me. Want them for the band, but, wonder if they'd even care? Don't think they'd even want me back. They're on their own, relieved I am not one of their own.

Especially Johnnie, little drummer boy. He thought I hated him. I loved him. Feel abandoned, inside. Though, I've felt worse. When I write in my diary, I'm doing alright, really. When I don't write in it, my quietness means I am majorly bummed. I keep longing for the sea, for the Amolfi Coast in Italy. Cliffs and ocean. Warm Mediterranean breezes. Wish to smell the gentle sea air.

Read her letter over and over…..looking for her sign, any sign, anyone. Miss her but miss Rose, even more. Want Pam, less.

Tonight, I tell Rose that she comes to Italy or I leave without her. I am finally prepared to be weaned from her care. I am strong enough in body, mind and soul to go it alone. I love her but hate this damn friendship. Want more. New candles, new roses, a new start, I'll tell her. Will she? I'm afraid, no.

Hardly hear, 'Doors fever' anymore. Radio only blares, Zeppelin, Cat Stevens. American Pie is cool. Live it up boys! Time is short! Seems I've been forgotten. Midnight struck and the devil took my soul back! Fickle fans. Knew it though. Not much lasts forever. Little even lasts for a moment in time. That's probably good.

Even what we've made into our gods, fade. Need new ones every now and then. New promises. We always create new gods. Always need more saints! Want some blues here on the radio. How I feel inside. Keep biting my nails. I have none left. Wrote a few numbers, some 'ol blues I've re-wrote a dozen times. Toss it in the river.

Well, soon she'll be home. The ultimatum. Rose will come, but either way I will go.

So, will she stay?

Or, is it no?

---------JDM

DIARY ENTRY #13

28, December 1971
300 A.M. - Rome, Italy
Sometimes, I fear the nova. I'm totally alone, totally nothing.

Nothing, just made from stardust in the midst of this vast universe? Sometimes, it's overwhelming! It can even be lonely for atheists without a god to direct the orbs during sleep. So, god-damn lonely! It'd be nice to have some god, better yet, some hot goddess out there.

Something to yell back at you when you yell at the night. Nothing, but dust!

Something about, '*sitting under the tree*.' Plato said we will live this life again and Again? Live each of our lives eternally. That the dream of our life we'll live over and over. My only consolation is that at the nova my dust will meet with the molecules of, Buddha, Confucius, Renoir, Einstein, Chopin, and, we'll all be reunited with each other in that spark. An eternity in a mille-second. Reunited again, like when we were created in the chaos. 'Till then we suffer the existential silence. Our fate.

Wishing to wake the dead, 315 in the morning now. Can't sleep. Only write. Maybe these words to give to my kid one day? Me, a father? A fucking joke, some accident or trap, some lure set by Rose, just as Eve lured Adam with her seductive fruit.

Past few days been pretty good. As good as it'd get. But, I leave the pension to meet my love only to be accosted by gypsies on the front steps. Little children, really. Holding signs at their waists, crowding me. Must have been a dozen of these little fucks. They're moving in for the kill, grabbing me, biting me, trying to pick pocket me, pulling at me.

Kick one, then two, in the shins. They scream, begin yelling and I run. Lose them in some medieval alley, an old labyrinth of brick houses not far from the Vatican. I can see St. Peter's dome at the end of the maze. They find me though, charge me again. Some ugly ass gypsy man comes out of the shadows, screams some Slavic or some mean shit at 'em for they run their asses off in fear.

He speaks to me in French. I shake my head, *no*. Then, German, shake it again, *no*. Italian, *no*. English, *yes*. We smile. Says he is so very sorry. Come in forsomething, please, please, he begs me. Has deep lines carved into his face like a roadmap. One hell of a life.

I have to meet my lover though, I tell him, can't go in, but he insists. Still have to get her a gift, Christmas Eve and she's crazy for that shit.

I am a little bit, no, I am very curious to go in, so, I go. She said 4, but, it's 5pm.

I look at her now sleeping on the couch. Says she loves it here. She must've awakened when I fell asleep, my snoring keeping her awake again, I am sure.

The gypsy man, *please*, he says. I show him one finger in the air. One minute I say! Only one, he says, yes, yes, he is pleased. Finally, I go inside hoping I don't die on Christmas Eve. Sit down, sit down he says. Everything he says, he says twice.

Twice as funny with his crooked mustache and big gut with shirt buttons opened by his belly button. Exposed skin. His greasy braided hair hangs like nooses. Really disgusting, but, kind of cool in a way. He is real, at least. I take the wine he hands me. I refuse to sit.

A woman, white milky cataracts, stares at me. Kind of startles me. Did not see her sitting there in the corner with her gray hair and bun-like hair-do. She blends in nicely with the smell and cockroaches and faded bright colors of some rugs on the walls. She speaks to me. I don't know what she says. The man says, she wants your palm. Your hand. Give it to her. The old man says, she can't bite! More wine? I shake my head, yes, he happier, she begins to feel the inside of my right palm. It tickles tracing the lines with her index finger. Mumbling. What's she saying, I ask. Her black mouth, no teeth inside, touted off three predictions he says.

I've always heard that death comes in three's.

The gypsy man with black hair, face and clothes translates for me as the old fortune teller does her thing. One, she says, *there is someone near you who overshadows you, someone who threatens your happiness but more importantly, even threatens your life.* Two, she utters sounds, *if I live a life of lies, how can I ever know the truth?* And, three, *she shakes her head, no,* won't tell him, can't tell me she says. What is it? We beg her. No, no, no, she says, takes my palm, closes it, pushes my hand towards my heart. He says she wants me to go now.

It's a dark room, musty, even moldy. She stares at me. I finally reach into my pocket giving her some twenty dollar bill. Funny how she sees that, she's happy as hell. I decline more wine from the man. For the road he says, drink up! To life! She's still sitting but now begins to take off the necklace she is wearing with a rounded cat's eye stone dangling. She puts it in my palm, closes my hand and begins to kiss my knuckles. I take it. She says in English, *protection, protection*! The room is silent, dead silent. Until the door busts open. Scares the shit out of me! 3 or 4 kids come running in with cardboard signs. Holy shit, it's them. They hand their papa, as they call him, some wallets, money, a watch. They all look so happy, even dancing. I check for my wallet, got it. Check for my watch, gone! I go wild, yelling!

The gypsy man lets me look amid their treasures. Surer than shit, they got mine. I take it and he says, please, please! I whip the middle finger in his face and shout, FUCK YOU! They are all laughing! Even the old woman! I grab the bottle of wine and whip it against the wall of brick in the room! It crashes, glass everywhere. Silence for a second, then, more laughing! I finally escape wondering what else I am missing. I run out of the house, lost now in the alley. Wonder where the café is from here. I can't help but wonder of her warnings. Bullshit, I think. Someone stands in the way of my happiness? My life? Who? It's after 6 now, I was to meet my soon to be wife two hours ago!

I feel crazed from the wine, running through the streets screaming, BULL SHIT! BULL SHIT! I'm in dire need to find the Café Allegro. Making up excuses in my head for when I see her. I have her Christmas gift in my hand, at least.

------JDM

DIARY ENTRY #14

I wonder sometimes…..can just anyone write or think like me? Or, is it something few have inside them? Am I really that unique?

"…why's beauty so timeless?
Love, so ageless…?"

She loved my, "gypsy gift" of the tiger's eye. I kissed her as I placed it around her neck. Told her, "it's for protection, protection." Had a little pizza, some beer, talked like we just met yesterday.

Merry Christmas, James! Merry Christmas, Rose! Though we had no snow we had some cold chills as we finally arrived at the Coliseum. Her favorite ruin in Rome.

"Once, I believed in a devil and once I offered to trade him my soul.
But, even he refused to take it, giving it back to me,
unlocking the powers I already possessed within me."

---JDM

Too bad the Romans didn't have more lions, I mumbled, knowing it would disturb her. She rolled her eyes. She always does that. I talked that religion was folklore, myth. That no Christians were ever fed to the lions. Only a way to evoke feelings in you to feel sorry for them and join them. But, she still wanted the mid-night Mass. I knew that she would not let go of that idea. I couldn't go. They'll do fine without me!

She said that my own music was very, "catholic." Good vs. evil. That the church's influences ran deeply through my blood. Amazing she would say that about my music. She never really knew much of me or my music until she rescued me. And, I am sure that she still knows very little. Finally, I agreed to her wish.

The papal mafia sang in Italian, and, I recognized the hymn, the words from when I was a boy, singing it in my church back home in Florida. Went like,

> *"...sons of God, hear his holy word, gather*
> *'round the table of the Lord.*
> *Eat his body, drink his blood.*
> *Then we'll sing a song of love..."*

I kept listening to the words inside me even after the singing had concluded. It was so sick, demented. Eating dead god's flesh to gain their power? Yet, for thousands of years man has done just that. When would we grow out of it? As the priest consecrated the bread holding up the round host in the air, an image of a Maya priest holding a virgin's beating heart in the air, consecrating his people to the deity, struck me.

Man makes his gods in his own image, and then worships them. How strange! The priest then drank some of the blood, as now the priest drank the wine. We call the ancient Maya cannibals, yet refer to the priest of today as holding the truth? Who needed a god when you had this religion? The people alongside me in the pew, the "faithful," were in a trance affixed by this magic. Hocus pocus put them on some journey, like some acid trip.

Rose whispered, "I know it's a myth, but, it's comforting," we smiled. I couldn't leave this tomb of the dead god soon enough.

From the church we went to a little restorante for Christmas dinner. Late, or, early as hell and dinner just begins in Italy.

It's great, too!

It was underground, under the streets was an ancient theatre. Felt like some tragic actor or dramatist here at, Contanza. Dark inside. Only candles. Brick walls, floor. Dark wooden table and chairs. Really very cool place. Sipped hot wine. Cracked our teeth trying to open roasted chestnuts. The morning hours lingered on, just talking.

So, what of your parents she asked again and again! She says don't say they're dead. I say, they're dead. We laugh. She begs me to begin with what she calls, "your story." I'm kind of feeling shit faced. From the wine here and from the wine I polished off at church! Bottles were beginning to line up on the table. Eating bread, waiting for our food, I lit another cigarette.

Everyone in here stares at my feet. Didn't they ever see sandals? "Hey, these are toes! I am Jesus Christ! Today's my birthday! Dig it?" I yell out to the place. Everyone is silent but then begin talking again. It is crowded like a son of a bitch in here. Some wine cellar of a grave under the earth. Rose continues to piss me off, "your story, James. Please, for me. Consider it a Christmas gift." I tell her that she got the eye. She is pissed now, I tell her my parents, Steve and Clara are dead. I'm an only child. The end!

She thinks I'm ruthless. I just know it. Play too many mind games with her. But, I love it. I can see it on her face. So, I begin as she moves in closer to hear me. My father was a priest. My mother a nun. I'm a bastard child. "*A bastard,*" she asks?

Her eyes widen, roll, her face frowns. Ok, ok, ok. Ok, but why does she have to know, even? But, I try telling her what I know. More like what I want to remember.

Born in Florida. Cute baby. Chubby cheeks, smartest little brat in the world. The horse that became the unicorn. I'm in love with my mom. I really care for her. She was good to me. Rarely saw my father. Don't mind that though. Hell, don't even know my dad. Travels a lot. Rimbaud's father did the same shit to him.

My family traveled all the time. Have some siblings, I suppose. They come along later. I'm like an only child really, feel like an only.

I read a lot growing up. Found a world I can live in there. An entire life to lead was always in words for me. It's hard to talk about myself, Rose! As hard as I try! I tell her. But, she wants to hear me too, even pouring me more wine. A first for her. Usually she is taking it away. Everyone in the joint speaking Italian, so damn fast, too. From drinking coffee? Their coffee pots flow all night. It looks like oil!

I think that maybe I was an adopted child 'cause I'm so vastly different from anyone in my family. Or, maybe I got switched to the wrong family? Hell, if I know. She wants to know what these parents then, my so called, real parents may have been like.

Hmmm, I think they're professors, or, explorers. Yes, my lost father is an oceanographer looking for the Titanic. And, my mother is an archaeologist looking for lost civilizations. She loves the Maya and lives most of her life in Mexico. I come back to reality, Florida was, ok. Had to grow up somewhere. That is as good as any I would guess. Yes, mam. No mam. All the formality I did not like there though. So fake, superficial. Felt like my dad's dead all the time growing up. A ghost who appears every now and then to make sure we move. I once counted that by high school I was in at least 5 different schools and 5 different states. Can't really have any friends that way. You make one, you just begin to like someone and you move. Why bother? It was shit!

As a boy, a child really, I already knew who I was. That I'd do something great or something evil one day. That I'd always be remembered for something. If biographers have written about the lives of great people throughout history, who would record my life? I always wondered, always felt this while growing up. Still feel it now, still wonder. But, I doubt in five years, since now everyone thinks I'm dead, that I will be remembered.

As a kid I read the Kafka diaries, loved them, was inspired to write mine when I was about ten. Began, then. Drew a lot of dirty ass pictures in them. Got a lot of ideas in them for some songs, even.

See, I was born during World War II. Raised during the Korean War. And, now I live in the Viet Nam War. My whole god damn life there's been a war going on, always a conflict greater and deeper inside me though. Probably why my blood is so red. Never seen anyone's blood redder than mine.

She seemed bored as I rambled, looked real bored. I began smoking a lot more of her cigarettes. Where the fuck was our food?

She then wants to know less facts and more about me. I don't get it. I kind of withdraw from her as I withdrew from the world as a kid. Back then I was really shy and quiet. She doesn't believe me. I was a hell of a good kid who was always writing. Lost in my own world. Alone a lot. That was when I was oh, maybe 9 or 10 I think. All that shit. Yeah, at 10 began my first poems. Never was happy with them. Like now. Would re-write them dozens of times. Like now. Wanted to say something but it seemed even words were never enough to explain my deepest feelings. Words are never enough! I mean I lived in this surreal world where the Grateful Dead and psychedelics ruled over me. My mind would never shut off. Like now. Never. Maybe all the drugs helped me? To calm me? I don't know. I know I hated TV as much as I do now, back then. The tube only speaks to the smallest of minds. Will ruin our civilization yet, wait and see.

I mean my wife Pam loved folk music. I hated the shit. But, I wonder if it's just another voice to listen to, some other way of speaking? It sure seems a hell of a lot more real than some dumb ass TV show portraying the perfect family. My ass!

I think that's why I was so rebellious in high school. I mean I was trying to be heard. Knew I had a message but no one'd listen. So, I would get up on a table in the cafeteria and yell it out! Scream, step on trays. No one else had the guts to do it. Only me. I'd would fucking curse out the school's so called authorities and 'tidy worlds' just to be heard. No one listened then, not listening now. How can anyone be heard?

See, in those poets like Rimbaud or say Baudelaire, or, even Blake, I saw that they were saying the same things I was trying to say. They said it 100 years earlier. No one was even listening to them. I heard them trying to be silenced back then too. Like me. That's when I knew I wanted to be just like them. I mean Nietzsche seemed as if he was speaking ONLY to me when I read him. I read any and all books I could find back then when I was say, 13.

When I read the poets or philosophers I felt like I was their only audience. I saw I was like them, someone who had inherited a destiny. I knew I was to change the world somehow. Make it greater than it was. Or, I would die trying.

The food had come. Couldn't recognize what it was, couldn't remember what we ordered. It all looks the same anyways. Red. Wine poured, I felt numb. I'd been telling her all. Think she liked it.

Lived a lot with my grandparents when I was in high school. Loved it. Back in St. Petersburg, Florida. They loved me, understood me like no one had before. Didn't think I was crazy or some bad ass wild child. They saw my vision.

Had a friend in school there, too. Got close, then we moved away. Finally, I left for college, FSU. My parents were pissed when I wanted to move to L.A. and do film school. Kiss my ass! I thought, what? Why the fuck would they care what I did in college? They're never there and all of a sudden they want to appear? Why they controlling my life?

If my dad was dead he would still try to run my life from the grave. Fuck that! Piss on it! I went. Hauled my ass to L.A. with a friend who drove there from Florida. Elvis fucking blasting from the radio. I mean man it was fucking beautiful! Really fucking beautiful!

In the desert I felt free, I mean when we hit east Texas I was home free! Totally alive! I was finally, free!

Loved New Mexico, once lived there. And, loved Arizona. We slept on the sand under the stars. Just me and the stars! Was great to get back out west, finally! I knew in an instant here's where my heart belonged. Ever had that feeling? That kind of connected feeling to something other than yourself? Rose said it with me, "holy shit!" The first and only time in her whole life she said that, I'm sure!

She wanted more of the fucking story. How much more could I tell? Burned the roof of my mouth on the hot cheese, could hardly talk. Just laughed for a while. For nothing. Silly shit. Laughing. *FUNG GU*, I yelled at my waiter and some freaks who kept staring at me. They notice me, I wonder?

I just told Rose that they're all dead. Even my brother and sister. All dead. I know no one anymore. I mean I never had a god-damn relationship with a god-damn one of them, that's why they're dead!

We talked more into the night. Seems night doesn't last as long as it once did. When I was a kid. Used to last forever it seemed. Surer than shit its dawn, it's light out, even the Eternal City comes alive to re-awaken.

Smell of fresh bread in the air. Shutters open slamming against the brick. People yelling, sound like they are fighting, only to say hello to some neighbor. Noisy trucks making deliveries, car horns, the atmosphere of life all ruined even underground, here.

She wanted to know more but told her there was no more to tell. End of story! I mean it's not some pretty picture, my life. Fuck that! From womb to tomb, I am born, die, and, hope that somewhere in between, I am able to live. I mean really live! That I'm not some automaton controlled by society, government, religion. Shit, can't escape their influence, they're making me paranoid. But, big brother does suck the life out of you if you let 'em. So maybe my music will outlast me?

The story of my life, what I did in my music can one day go on and on even without me? It's what I wanted. Like picking up some Kafka diary, someone can hear in my music my diary. An era's sentiments of the people. The real people. Not just some fucking propaganda made up by the lying ass people in power. That they'll hear a history of how it really was in 1970, how it really was in my days. Not just some fucking lying version or some distorted facts. I have a feeling that I just might endure.

'Cause, in the end there'll always be music and in music they'll always be words and feelings. The truth. Just like it was in the beginning. We can win out over them. Our real story will survive through music. Since the time when we lived in caves we made music. We'll never stop even if the Soviets nuke us or if we nuke them first. Think we will nuke them first.

I can only imagine there being a nuclear war. My ass, this will someday end! This race for power! We'll crawl from the rubble and keep making our music, telling our story.

In the end there will always be music, maybe not me. But, music! 'Cuz music is bigger than my life, a whole lot bigger than life. Shit, we've already won.

----------JDM

DIARY ENTRY #15

Hitting rock bottom emotionally, these poems were all writ during an, *'induced state.'* Alcohol, opiates, or both. French wines, Russian vodkas, ruby ports and Amaretto de Serrano. Potent pain killers.

A *'toxic concoction'* mixed with phobias of a poet losing his life at any moment, inspired them. So did insomnia and the reading of other poets.

With a *'toast'* in one hand, and a pen in the other, the poet spent many a dark hour working. Little to no remembrance of writing them does this poet have.

Months after their finish the poet *re-discovered* them. The poet read, re-read and began to memorize them. Clutched them to his breast during sleeping hours. Carried them throughout the day. They became a source of comfort, an act of solace on the path of, *existential recovery.*

In celebration of the new year those musings from little scraps of paper, little notes, many scribblings, flow below. 'Cause I am that poet!

Here's those lonely pleas during those hopeless nights prior dawn.

Jim Morrison
Firenze, Italy
1972

DARK NIGHTS PRIOR DAWN

One day shall it be. Alone, with all my rot.
Open, then close.
Grave for the tomb lie deep within, cold, dark.
Like the womb.

Here, death only ages.
Bones ravaged, consumed as night.
Flesh only a once! Cross saves us not.

----------JDM '72

Life, you come to tempt, but never to stay.

Cursing my fate I curse you more.
Damn life most.

--------JM

Tranquilize my fate? Words don't suffice me!
Only closer to the soul do I become.
In dire despair I seek potent relief.
Seek some day when life will share its secrets,
say to me,

"death shall never come."

----JM 1972

Winds soar speaking turbulently,
as in heart I too, soar.

And, souls speak. Telling much of life yes,
but, most of love more.

-----Jim Morrison

Crisis of the life.
Cries of our death.

In this world great pain.
My songs spread more?

Let the nova judge.
Let not my life pass away, alone.

-----James d. M'son 1972

Beautiful forms danced before me, upon the light.
Eyes beheld beautiful spirits.

Souls touched as once, too, you fled.
Love was not me. Was not you.

-------JDM

Madness looms.
In my voice music sings.

Poems sing in memory of days when I longed for love.
Now, life has gone, though, really never really come.

Weep tears.
Cry so loud.

Wish only for the past to come and take me away.
Take me back.

Take me back to you.

----JDM

Wishing not for desolation. As if through some poison. There's a way
to end this abyss of pain.
I would.
But, I can't.

No one my way has been of grace.
Has come from the grave to touch me , true.

-------JDM '72

Life's end, speak of it not.

Soft pillows, dream of such more.

Love is not friend, nor foe.

True, in life one lives only to die.
If only in death one loved to live life more.

------Jimbo

I look for days when nights turned chills to wine.
Now, longing, I lament, only to wish life was not so cruel.
And, death was not the inevitable.

-----J. M.

Life goes on. Fading as the sun.
No where am I upon this earth?

My bones only as dust nearer to stars each day?

Echoes came as voice.

--------Jim M.

Wind, speak not in silence.
No one hears your voice.

Intimations pour forth.
Libations fill spirits in my empty glass.

Fine wines told of love coming to be.

Cold winds,
empty streets,
dark nights
scream!
Just now no one will listen.

-------JDM

Listening to winds I soar as trees.
Float as the leaf.

With wounds of war I wore my scar.
Reliving the gentle good night,
I die.

Jim Douglas Morrison, 1972, Italia

If you were near my muse would you be.
Graveyards speak.

From below.....yours the name I call.
From above....yours the name I hear.

----J Did all!

Intercede not of days long past when I thirsted for life.
For then unaware was I of death.
Yet, long only for moments when pain came not.

When the earth would promise not to swallow me up,
and, then, spit me out.

----------J rocks M----1970's

Lament.
Pine.
Long I do.

Not for beauty. Not for love.
But for you!

-------Jim's M'rson '72.

The wish to sleep.
Enjoy moments of peace my dream.

Oh, repose, sing to me.
Sing the praise of sleep,
Of rest.
A lullaby of solace.

Oh, restful night forever must I remain against the cold night
as
restless?

-----Son of Steve, James. 1972.

Numb, no feel.

None of the feelings touch me.
Two times, madly.

Not for day, nor night.
Long only for you.

------Jim Morrison, 1972,

Avec:

Europa and the Bull = Jimmy & Love

DIARY ENTRY #16

Got home busted and bruised and bleeding. 'Nother bar fight, mother fucks! Wanted snake skin. That fucking simple! Ain't got any! My ass! I seen it slithering! Won't sell it? I'll take the leather, but I don't wear leather. Leather wears me, possesses me. My soul compliments it.

Then, Rose's nowhere to be found. Or, found out. I never find her here anymore. Lip's bleeding, still! No bandages. No one to help! Inside, the place is lonely and dark. God-damn! Outside it's rainy and night's just begun. She fights a lot with me here, more lately than ever. I bow in silence, no spectators, no fans or crowds! Damn!

THE LIZARD KING IS HERE!

Finally, all alone! My magic's ever near!

I'm the Lizard KING! I can do ANYTHING!

No one ever cheers!

-----JDM

DIARY ENTRY #17

Florence, Italy

Don't fucking get it!

Amid the back drop of the war all this happy go lucky music blares! The beach. Free love. Sunshine. Trips. Happy together. Bubblegum always playing on the radio as napalm rains down on people!

It's like no one cares that the Viet Nam war is even going on. It's like no one knows that the President is in on a major conspiracy! One day, that crooked king will be no more! Nixon'll burn his own ass, yet! Just watch and see!

The nukes could fly, hit D.C. We spray agent orange on people in Viet Nam. We kill our own people. And, still, that shit keeps playing? I mean America could fall! So, fuck it! Let it! But, people need not hide, escape their fears by running to shallow music made of sugar!

We need some good thinking songs made out of blood. My songs need to be heard now! Shit, more than ever!

And, they don't even call it a war! It's only a "conflict." Like some 50,000 dead GI's from the USA and a million of 'em from Nam and that's not a war? Seems everyone's oblivious to this atrocity. Their flowers and riots and protests don't work. Need more, need me. Mojo's vision to end it all.

Don't get it. Just don't.

Feed the pigeons in the city squares nowadays. Instant friends. More pigeons here than dead artists or war dead. Even today you gotta die to be great! SHIT man! Just don't get it!

Train from Rome was cool. Tuscany great! Rolling hills, pretty cool! Rose and I on endearing terms again, got a place with a great view of Florence. From above, looking down, the Arno slips on by looking up to our windows. A thin sliver of a river, it is. But, I still long for the sea. Any sea I want to see. Smell the salty air more.

Pure gold on the domes and towers shine under the sunshine here. Spectacular view! Exactly what she wanted.

Every footstep taken here takes you back a hundred years! It's pretty much a romantic place, revitalizing our love, perfect place for a marriage, she says. If she says so, let her.

Radio news, now. Heard that some grieving fans committed suicide over me a while back. Totally fucked! Heard they're conducting séance's just to contact me. Hell, give me a call! I'm right here! Not in the ether! Shit, just call! Would love to talk!

Read a lot here, write a lot, but not as much as I'd like. Looking in little nooks and crannies in this old city most of the time. Other day followed this old cobble stone street in the opposite direction of the tourists. Tourists drive me nuts! So, I get away. And, it's quaint and quiet. Lots of little shops, a café, lots of cool places making all their shit by hand. And, quiet! Just don't see a soul.

I walk down this sidewalk and hear this music playing. I see some place with a door kinda open. Kind of like it's calling me to go on in. The music sounds like angels. Some choir. Thought I died and went to heaven. Too, unlikely. I walk closer and closer. Want to go on in.

The heavy doors creaks as I open it wider, peaking in. That music's in there. What's this place I say to myself. I walk inside. It's ever so dark in here. So, I see nothing.

Eyes adjust and I see its some old chapel, some old church, just falling apart and kind of in ruins. Damp, roof leaking, drops of water hit my head. The walls are rock, the floors too. No windows. Just walls. Dark inside 'cept for a few dying candles. The music is some record player, I find. I walk around, wondering. Kind of cool in here. Suddenly, it's my room with one hell of a view!

I walk over to a side altar to see the grave under it. A woman lying on top of the floor, a dame made of marble. I move in closer, grab a candle. She's supple. Fresh. Looks real, alive. I brush off this plaque on the floor. I read it. Hard to see. I can't believe what I've found or what's found me. It's great! It's Beatrice. The exact same Beatrice the great poet Dante loved, but never met! And, Dante wrote the most beautiful poetry in our civilization! And, to her. He immortalized her!

Dante wrote, *The Inferno!* And, poems to Beatrice. Says this place is where he first saw her, fell in love with her, was inspired to write poetry for the very first time. He never spoke to her, only bumped into her walking in here once at those creaky doors I just came in through.

He never knew her but really loved her. Loved her more than most people love the ones they see. It's easy to love a person. But, hard to love an ideal, someone, something you've never met. People say it's easier to love the ideal. No Way! Not for me, not for Dante. 'Cause nothing ever measures up to your ideal. Those who love the deepest, only sabotage any hope for real love, true love! Just like me, just like Dante. They're doomed!

I'll never forget reading Dante in high school. My teacher making us memorize a line of his. I'll never forget the line either,

> *"...there is no greater pain than to remember*
> *a happy time when one is in misery..."*

Dante watched her every move. Watched her marry in here, his heart broken. Heard of her early death. Attended the wedding and the funeral. And, they never spoke. She never knew the deep love he held for her, she never knew of the poems he wrote of her. Poems considered to be as great as Shakespeare's. I'm overwhelmed just being here. I lay down next to her.

Didn't know the place even existed. Must not be in their tour guides. Thanks for that! But, here it is. Here I am. Alone. Only that music. No one around here in that noisy city either. No one. Just me.

I was led here, drawn here by Beatrice. Now she knows what Dante did for her, knows of the poems, knows how he immortalized her. That record ends but begins again and again, automatically. Who starts it even? Heard this record a dozen times. I mean I just happened upon this place. Am I the only one who knows of this treasure, this marvel?

Here, at this very spot Dante was inspired by her to write his poetry. Here, I feel I've met the greatest poet ever and the greatest of lovers ever! Here, two great poets met: Dante and me!

I felt the breasts of the marble Beatrice. Want to lay on top of her. Feel her lips, kiss the soft marble, lick her cheeks. Wish to make love to the rock. I hear someone coming. I lay flat on my stomach. Bow to their 800 year old love. Someone changes the record. I want to hear, *The Doors*. Want to play it for her. Wish it to be, *The End*. Not a chance. They leave, as soon do I. But now it's pitch black in here, ever so dark. But, I see it all.

So, now, I'm kind of silent, kind of reverent for hours. Spellbound. I drink some Irish coffee in this cozy little square by the Uffizi art gallery.

I'm protected from the moonlight's lure of love by a simple umbrella. I won't even tell my 'find' to Rose.

Want this all to myself. My secret.

My thirst quenched. For, now!

-------JDM

DIARY ENTRY #18

14, February, 1972
St. Valentine's Day
Firenza. Italia.

Feels like spring here! Think of Amsterdam a lot. Plenty of reefer, sex, red lights. All legal, too! All just waiting for me, calling me, tempting me with the smell of its' allure. Mmmm. Nice! Sweet! Still searching for omens!

Rose says, "no." It's too rude. Too insulting. Too damn bad then! She won't go to Amsterdam? I long for decadence more and more, lately. The blond beast prowling?

Tonight, she proposed to me, I said, "I do." She said you don't say "I do," except on the wedding day. I asked Rose then what do I say now? She says you say, "yes." I give her a big, "yes." One in French. One in Italian, even one in Dutch. No rings. Just kisses, happiness. She happier than me. Long time in coming, though I knew it was coming.

Don't like to make a bond of love, though. Who needs the law to say we're in love? To pledge an oath of love is fine. Like with me and Pam. But, to wed?

Rose wants a honeymoon in Venice. Me, in Amsterdam. Got her some flowers, but, really wanted to put them next to Beatrice. Still haven't lost my little rectangular shades. Everything looks orange through them. The world is orange! It's an orange world! Wow! How profound! Got an earring. Hurt like hell!

Love this funky beatnik look, real Bohemian feel to me, inside and out. Feel cool, feel trendy. Digging it to death! Rose hates it! That's why I love it more!

I'll love her to death do us part, just don't fence me in. Want, long for large open spaces in love. In life. Can't be caged in. Like some bird I can't sing. Singing's my life, too.

Rose's so mysterious, so solid. I lean on her but don't really know her. I don't ask. She never tells. Soft exotic skin, red lips, long auburn hair. My black Venus. In bed, I recite love poems in her ear. She says she remembers them all. It's like she's a mother, a sister, a wife, a friend. But, all in one!

Kinky to vanilla, this woman rocks, always elevates the bed from the floor!

She understands me and never says, "if you loved me you'd stop this." Or, "you'd do that." Gonna tie the knot at that Dante church. No minister, just some notary or lawyer will do. Don't think that lawyer speaks English. That'll be a scream, a riot!

I'll tell her about the history of the Beatrice place after we're wedded. Surprise her inside there.

Tru luv.
Beauty, heart, mind and soul.

Yes, tru luv.

Wherever it leads,
wherever I may roam.

---------JDM

I'll read this poem to her tonight in bed. She seems more and more androgynous looking, lately. Actually, so many people do. I see someone and I wonder, man or woman? I keep asking what they are as I peer onto them. Boy or girl? Infants and babies look sexless. So do really old farts. So do most people. Rose. Even, me!

Sometimes, when I look into the mirror I can't tell about my own looks. My own features make me wonder if I look like a man or a woman?

Feel dizzy now. Head spins. Room flies on by.

Walked on by the Palazzo Vecchio today and its square. On the square's floor there's this gold plaque I found. This priest Savanarola was burned exactly there 500 years ago. Went nuts over nudity. Got lots of painters to burn their nudes as he deemed them evil. Sinful in the eye of the god, he said. Even talked Botticelli into burning some of his art, too. Couldn't help but piss on his marker. Nuts! Should have burned HIM sooner. What is that they say, something like, '*those who burn books soon burn minds?*' Man, free us from the morally pure, lest they burn us in the name of god. Crazy fucks!

Oh, if Adam and Eve were created out of the mud, since then they were never born, did they have belly buttons? Always wondered that!

See, I love Rose but I hardly know her. She knows me more than I know myself. Perhaps she reads these very pages about herself? Nah, she promised not to.

Wedding on , March, 21st. The first day of spring, and, her birthday!

Oh, saw Michelangelo's, *David*. She loves the nude body. Loves the male nude. I love nudity more, though. She walks behind the towering, *David*. "Nice ass," she starts off. I say to her, "thanks hun!" She goes on, "no, not you!" Says, "well, yes you but him," pointing to his six foot cock! I lick my lips, jump up touching his ass. Some guard yells, "cusee, cusee." I act dumb. Say something like, "no speaka the Italiano my deara sira." He leaves but keeps an eye on me.

"You're going to get me kicked me out of here," she says. She's kind of serious. You should be so lucky I tell her. Rather get burned alive like old Savanarola. She laughs! Rolls her eyes. Tell her how I love the mind of artist-warriors!

Michelangelo believed in the humanity inside the stones he was working on. His chisel set the figure free. The form was always inside the piece of marble, like slaves crawling out from the rocks. It's cool that Hindus believe rocks are primitive souls. One of the first steps in reincarnation. I mean, I was so inspired with what I saw today, but, more with what I felt.

Most people here miss it all. Never see that rocks are just tears shed by mountains, mountains which once saw the abuse of an arrogant mankind.

We get something to drink. I get some cappuccino. Small cups, powerful brew. I zoom all day and night long on those demons. So does the rest of Italy! Shit, man!

Some punk offers to sell us some small white packet on the way home. "I'd rather have a drink than a drug anyday," I tell him. And, tell him to get lost. Long for one now.

Ask Rose if the days seem longer lately. Night so short? Not to her. Miss the night life with the band less and less. Though, crave the fame more.

We walk past a few of my bars, hangouts. Then, come up by one near the church of San Croce. We stroll arm and arm on by. See this priest on the steps of the church just sitting. Long brown robe. White rope hanging down on the side and around his waist. See his pants, socks, and shoes under the robe from how he sits. Pack of cigarettes in between his sock and shoe. He lights up. I know the dirty face. Know that bushy stash on his face from somewhere.

"Ah, you're no man of the cloth I tell him! You're Roberto," I yell. Rose says for me to stop. But, it's true! He comes running towards me. "Jimmy, Jimmy, si, si," he carries on, hugging me, practically kissing me. He's my damn ass drinking buddy! Guzzles the most I've ever known of anyone and has got a mouth on him like a sewer.

"Got a tourist group a coming, a soon, Jimmy! Gotta do my little a song and dance! Gotta put on a show you know!" Then he says, "how else can I afford my habit without a part time job?" Can't help but loving this and rolling in laughter. Puts out the cigarette as he prayerfully bows his head, his hands folded, walking up the steps to the smiling tour group. He begins with, "welcome my dear children, Father wants to…"

I'm still laughing. Rose shakes her head trying not to laugh. "Come on, laugh! Laugh!" Finally, she busts out laughing, dying! Says she did not want to laugh and encourage me.

Sure hope to see him at the bars soon. Now, that kindly old padre owes me a drink. Make mine a double!

------JDM

DIARY ENTRY #19

She longs for Venice. Me, Amsterdam. She seems to be gone more and more. I wanted a dog. She did not. Sage, his name. Same name of my dog when a boy. She wants the mountains and I long for the sea. Black and white. Night and day. Vinegar and piss. Says I talk to people who aren't even there. That I sleep around. Never come home. Disappear for days. I tell her that's what's good about me. She's not amused.

Poppies at the Sea.
In them I am free.
Paper oranges flow unto snows of white.
Where fields of black speak of interior blues.
Never of skys, lately.
Poppies at the Sea.
In me, tears begin to see ...
they gave birth to the seas.

----------JDM

See heaps of dead corpses in huge piles from the plague around the city here. No one sees them? And, no one burns the piles? I try to tell people to burn the bodies. It's the only way to kill the disease, not burial. Can't burn the bodies, Roman pagans did that? Church can't be pagan? Only burial is the way, they all say! Push me away. Think I'm drunk or crazy.

And when he lifted his head, perhaps to pray, no one was there.
And, in an age when no one knew, no one cared,
meaning was given to the mass by an institution. The church.
One which cared for power, it's 'secret' ulterior motive.
Cared for salvation,
but power was their god.
---------JDM

79

Just wanted to live on skid row under the bridges, I tell her. Under the Ponte Vecchio. I wanted to be with the bums, the real artists of Florence, the left over ones.

I won't sleep with her anymore. Maybe won't even on our wedding night. Yet, how I love her. How I hunger, thirst for her beauty, her soul.

She won't talk to me 'cept to tell me of the wedding. "Whose getting married," I ask? "Jim please," she finds no more humor.

She's become the usurper of my powers. Some capitalistic queen with a septre of greed. Pam has my last will and testament. Rose wants none of that, she says. Can't believe it. We argue. I stay away more, but do want like hell to marry her.

Yet, I just want to be alone. Know she saved my life. Just want some life. Can't find any now, especially not in a band. Tried to buy a gun today. For safety. For protection. To save myself. Not a one here.

Can't find Sage lately. She says the dog doesn't like me, why he ran away.

I drink all night, sleep all day. What does she do all night? She disappears all day.

Have I gone mad? Or, reached some intellectual nirvana like Nietzsche? Soon my coma will come like his? I should be so lucky.

"See you tomorrow at noon. At the church," she shouts. Door slams as she walks out, "don't you dare be late!"

I yell, "guess I got me a date?"

--------JDM

DIARY ENTRY #20

Finished reading, *A Moveable Feast*. Hemingway knew Paris then, but, I know Paris now. I long for that Paris when Rose and I once danced under the fountains wet pipes from our 'hide 'n seek.' Kissing in love, wiping back tears. It seems so long ago those little strolls through the Tuileries' palace gardens. Our long talks in the endless parks. I was alive then. Oh, how in her did my soul come alive!

Hand in hand we window shopped for fashion, perfumes, shoes. Sharing the finest of foods at the outdoor cafes. We'd dance in the rain then visit our favorite Chagall, Degas and Dali's. We love art!

She was my beautiful Renoir, blossomed into life. Like art, I'd always say, "you're exquisite."

In her were my needs fulfilled. She opened a newness to Paris for me. Never before did I embrace such city charm.

Imitating Rodin's, *Thinker*, we'd snack on escargot sold on the street. Loving the sweet smells of garlic butter. Our hopes were of visits to Vienna, Prague, Budapest. Plans were made for Egypt and Mexico.

She almost fainted when I flipped off Napoleon in his tomb. Laughed, when I threw coins at the silly tourists down below on their boats of Seine. Ran, when I set some birds free at the street markets. I had finally found love. And, she was the goddess Venus who ruled my world, until dawn.

Rose slipped on Monet's bridge losing a shoe in Giverny's pond. We laughed 'til we cried. There, I put wisteria in her hair, roses on her lips. She loved flowers. So we ran through the flower markets sniffing tons of fragrances until we could smell no more.

Lugged big 'ol antiques into her Paris flat, up and up and up the never ending steps. *Don't they have elevators in France*, I'd ask her? She'd smile and answer, *'no monsieur*,' almost dropping the heaviest hope chest on my foot.

Our creameries for cheeses and butters. Our patisseries for bread and cakes. Our brasseries for beer and wine. We lived on chocolate, beer, cheese and bread. Everyone there knew us, loved us. The was nothing that could go wrong while we were in Paris. How in Paris had we found life, had our hearts became as one.

I think that I can almost remember smelling her hair above me after her picking me off the street half dead. I do remember pretending while in her bed to be asleep and that very first touch. I still remember it. I do.

She nursed me back to health with her love, led me to goodness. She made her house into a home and I danced on in. It was love at first sight for me. Later, she said for her too. A shell had broken and out of it a romantic was awakened. Me!

With Rose, I did not feel like some filthy freak on stage. Not just defined by what I did. With her I was all I had hoped to be. I was who I was becoming, less of who I'd been. She saw the spark within and lighted me with flames of desire!

How could love which felt so right go so wrong?

After she found me, on the street in Paris, she dragged me into her place. And, when I first opened my eyes, finally seeing her, I had never seen such beauty, beauty which I wished not to defile, but to consummate. Our love making even drawing blood.

I listened to her dreams, held onto each word. I was genuinely interested in her life, cared less and less for mine. Now, we were to be wed. Here in Florence, Italy.

Beatrice was the bride of honor. Dante, my best man. The great day had arrived as I longed for it in our meeting on that very first day. Back in Paris.

The Dante Church! Bells rang! Pigeons ate rice, flew! Everywhere little yellow flowers glowed. Her birthday, my wedding day. Just seconds away.

Bad luck to see her face. I waited my turn. Classical music poured from outside the door. Vivaldi for sure played on. She inside in white. Virgin and pure to no one but me.

Curious onlookers pouring inside, passerbys lost in a crowd, outside. They tolled the bells just for us. Soon, twelve had rung. Or, was it just noon? Finally, time delivered me here. Shouldn't it be Pam?

I walked on by never to look in, never bringing a ring. I walked on by lost in a crowd, wishing for Paris again, dreading this bond. The flower falling, the Rose wilting. She standing alone. Me, finally free. Like the birds up above, freely flying.

A marriage made in heaven? Now, that's the divine comedy. Just read 'em and weep...

So, today I can say I finally saw the Beatrice who never knew of her Dante.

--------JDM

DIARY ENTRY #21

Chinese, Japanese, dirty knees,
Siamese...twins in their symbiotic
world float, like Krishna, above us!

Watching, looking, suspended by gravity.
Whims and desires raise all gods!

Transcending all voices, I hear Kali speak:
"...Free Tibet, land of our brothers, our
sisters, friends of Vishnu...."

Inside me, I listen:

Fire pours like rain.
Hearts break as glass.

In all a world,
this time's only a once?
Comes only to now, to this?

Fear not death,
just living no more.

Comes down to wishing for you,
only for you..."

------JDM

DIARY ENTRY #22

I expected her back but she never came.

In the morning, she was gone.

Listened to her music. Though she played it all the time, I don't remember ever hearing it. Lipstick on coffee cups. Strands of hair on her brush. Her scent locked within these walls. To Paris had she fled? Sputnik's beatnik?

Ruined hopes, broken dreams.

Shattered lives.

Unable to live, I tire, I wonder,
I die.

-----------JM

Imagined those long fingers playing piano back there, ivory keys matching her smile's teeth.

I had stopped loving this place wishing to leave my Florentine home for good. Now, only a house.

Thought I'd go crazy today. Thought I heard a blood vessel in my head explode.

This music montage of record titles from Mozart to Beethoven, she's left behind, is so soft. I listen to such heart wrenching music. Was the music coming from my heart of playing on the record player? It evokes such deep emotions in me, draws me to her, pulls me in deeper.

In her desperate hours did she feel like this too? Listen to the same pieces I hear now? I just never heard it playing. This is what she never shared? Now, I see, but my eyes are gone. Now, I walk in my own dark shadows like Oedipus. Now, I see how she dreamt. I dream her dreams, see her visions. Yet, without her.

How ever so perfectly did we drift apart, grow apart. Orchestrated so wonderfully like some opera's aria of torment and pain. My Madame of butterflies.

We stood in the way of each other's growth. She never knew me. I was the phantom of the opera in her life. Repression is the hardest form of denial. Ambivalent to caring and love, I was then. And, still am now.

A loud crescendo inside my head bursts out, "FUCK!"

Love is not real. Love is only sex disguised by society's permission called, love. We still feel guilty over that apple but in love our guilt feelings can disappear. For a while at least. Women the weapon. The vice still tempting men.

I will find her. I will. Make it up to her.

But, what if love gets in the way of life? Do I pass up life for love? Or, pass on love for life, instead? Life should be love but when it is not……damn if I know anymore!

Her leaving really bugs me. But, my own stupidity bugs me more. Putting her love into perspective in the scheme of my whole life this should not bother me one bit. I shouldn't mind. But, god it does.

Sociopath. Psychopath. I honestly seem to care so little. Heartless, gutless, am I.

The room's silent now, the music's over.

But, in life I still seek Spain's absinthe, that glowing green goddess, that seductive lure. Waiting for the sun and Pamplona's running of the bulls, those fights. Want to cheer standing next to Picasso for the matador's honor. Our Spanish caravan.

Want to lay in the opium dens of London, float in the dead sea, stand under Giza's pyramid.

God-damn! I missed her while I was looking for myself!

Next time I'll propose to her myself. Find her a ring. Will find her yet.

I've never heard the quiet before sound so loud as in this hollow room. No music, no soul.

If anyone could've changed me it would have been her.

-----JDM

DIARY ENTRY #23

Back up through the Dolomites, the Alps, little Swiss villages, Lake Como. When I awakened I was in Holland. Land of windmills and canals. Home to Amsterdam with the legal decadence I've craved. Here, everyone speaks English. Felt the cold ocean breezes sweeping across tulip patches down from the North Sea. I'm at the *Hotel Quentin*, looking down on a canal. Several stories up, nice view, but, had enough of views for a while.

Outta my mind already. Promised myself not to write of her, think of her. Still looking for her, though. Tired, settled down at this new place. Love it, love the city more. Talk in my sleep. Sleepwalk too, look out my window dreaming of her, wanting to jump. Nightmares abound.

Mormons, two by two, put their best foot forward selling levels of heaven, lots of wives and your own universe. Such a deal. But, prayers and sacred books and super hero gods tire me. Just placebos, opiates for the emotionally weak and the intellectually impoverished. These Jesus freaks trying to break up the fun in Amsterdam or something?

NOT a fat chance in hell!

----JDM

DIARY ENTRY #24

Not to be totally aware of what happens here each day is to not be alive! Something awesome, something very unique, beyond the realm of inspiration gives birth each and every day here. Artists, poets, musicians, thinkers, all assemble to partake in the feast that mainstream society denies. That being: <u>the expression of the self</u>.

Here, you can be free, think free, live free. At home when the high school bullies became tomorrow's cops, here, you see no cops. No real need for any. People get along fine here. All of life is legal here so no one need be arrested for breaking laws. I mean people here are decent. You help someone out with no place to stay or give someone a little money, you make a friend for life. Seems most people here just want to talk and be themselves. No one is violent, no one wants to hurt anyone else. Peace is the aim of life here. Why is that so hard to have anywhere else?

Amsterdam leaves its mark on all nations. People from all over the world come here. You can talk to people from China about their country. Laotians from Laos, talk to Germans from Germany. People are open minded, laid back, cool. Everyone wants to talk and talk about their homes and what it's like there. One thing we all have in common is that we love it here. I mean it's, GREAT!

Everyone just wants to join in this global experience called life. And, it's cool. Just like I envisioned it to be.

But, why must it only exist in Amsterdam?

----JDM

DIARY ENTRY #25

Fratricidal decadence is war. Fought by boys, for boys.

Real men think, use minds to avert conflict. Search deep to compromise, save lives.

King's heads must roll.

They seek neither.

"...stars, always still.
Almost near to touch.
Nearly.

Let kindness be my guide.
Only light my charm.

For, when you are lost,
you take my hand.

Guiding the way..."

The highest form of intelligence is compassion.
Second, is passion.

------JDM

DIARY ENTRY #26

Sparks snap and pop above you. Street cars zip everywhere. Neat bells ring on board them, too. Few autos. Go from place to place on electric! So buzzed out. Lots of theatres here, concerts, bar bands, poetry readings. Coffee and tea houses all over. You name it, you'll find it here. And, not too hard to do, either.

"As night's fallen, moon so full, your memory
fell across my face.

A comforting memory.

A very beautiful face."

----JDM

Talk to a lot of *posers* here. Those who only call themselves thinkers or writers, or musicians. They only think they're great. Sometimes, I think they only think they think. If you wanna be a writer, then write. Be a philosopher, philosophize. Wanna be a poet, then, feel and write deeply. For if you don't you only be the greatest wanna be on earth. Few get this truth, sadly.

But, I've found some people who seem to be real, authentic. Hate plastic faces and superficial existences.

Like these European people here, they seem to be the real friends I needed. Most of us just wander aimlessly through life, alone. Few even know they're alive. Walking zombies. No one thinks. Can't take that? Need others to talk with! To talk about things like this. That is meaningful living.

Got a bag tonight, the best shit I have ever had in my life. Ever! Weed not from some exotic place like India, or Cuba, but, from the Cumberland Plateau in Tennessee! Travel around the world for the best shit when some mountain folk down the road from me could of smoked me out a bowl. Bizarre, but cool! Love to meet 'em, visit that mountain! Party with them one day!

So, we all talk. Sit on the brick street corners smoking pot. Talk, talk, talk. About life, death, love. Hate and war. Wonder out loud we do. It's a real magnet for those of depth and meaning. Never talk of Rose with them. But, always think of her. Have to remember to forget. But, can't.

No one here knows who I am. Which I wanted. Just see me as a friend like I see them. It's cool. Radical. We get to the bottom of things. Or, at least die trying. Cool dudes, cool chicks. Very hot chicks for dinner every night! It's all OK here, no moral barriers.

Smoke a lot of dope lately, but, hey, it's Amsterdam, man! Makes me think! Feel a lot more that I wouldn't usually feel. At least they're not planning to ban people's thoughts or ideas here. Or, stop our thinking minds. Find a lot more tea houses here than coffee shops. Fine with me. Instead of tea leafs some places use marijuana leafs. Tasty and potent too! Dig it! Drink that and green and white teas most. Guy says try the teas without sugar. So, I do. Seems we cover the taste of the tea with sweet. Not a lot of space to sit down in these tea houses. But, it's worth the wait.

They play a lot of Dylan here. Some Yardbirds, sometimes even, The Doors. Makes you think and ponder your fate. Never heard them play the Doors before until today. Going to ask for more of my music!

Decent dudes here dragged me to a play. Didn't want to go. Not even with some hot chicks. But, I went. It's Wilde they said, DORIAN GREY. I said WILD! It's so damn great!

Seems I forget a lot lately. Fall asleep a lot. But, I'll never forget Dorian Grey stabbing the painting of himself as he suddenly falls down dead. His real face turns from young to old at that moment. Like Wilde was saying, well, like King Midas, *all you touch turns to gold*. Great, but you touch food and it's gold. So, your gift kills you, your greatness destroys you. I think of my life, my career, like that often. It's like all these mottos or parables are in my life here, speaking to me everywhere.

They make me think. Must be here for a reason?

Talk for hours of that with them. Keep thinking of Dorian Grey. He only wanted to be beautiful. Loved. Like me only wanting fame. Kick the shit out of the world's authority! That's all. Then, Dorian gets it and he doesn't want it anymore. Like King Midas, like me. *Be careful what you wish for! You just may get it!* But, it's so true. You want, want, want. You want something so much in life. It's all you think of. Then, you finally get it and you don't want it anymore. Didn't know it would be like that for me, a burden.

Life's so weird, so confusing. Seem I know all the answers in life one second then I don't know anything the next. I only have a magnitude of questions, lately.

> *"Magnitude, longitude, altitude.*
> *Think straight, feel free, dudes!*
> *Latitude, servitude.*
> *Be not a slave to yourself,*
> *dudes!"*
>
> ----JDM

Seems I cry a lot lately. Feel alone. Think even more. Like Dorian Grey, I crave beauty. Like a bitch in heat, a vampire lured by blood. Want beauty to possess my heart. Can beauty and heart ever be as one? Must all the beautiful ones be empty? Only pretty faces with nothing to say?

Why must the ones of depth always be so ugly? The evil sorcerer god again? Trickster of a god? Rather have a genie in a bottle any day than that kind of god!

Days go by. Nights too, pass me over. Spend a lot of time checking out this very cool city. Exploring a lot. But, it seems in every nook and cranny, every brick or in the mortar, I find myself more.

God, need to crash. Feel like I am flying on some rainbow now. On some beam of cosmic light. I must be walking in the very center of the universe. No more words left...anymore. Amsterdam's even taken my breath away.

----JDM

DIARY ENTRY #27

Unable to write. I fight to create. The rains pour as I write to loud claps of thunder. Listen to Rose's, *Verdi Requiem*. Music for the dead. It's cool. I have found in my life consolation, which I crave from time to time.

On nights as these, in a life as this, I fight for my immortality.

----JDM

DIARY ENTRY #28

Behind bars nefarious leviathans swim. In public natatoriums they utter their songs.

My pauper prince, not so little, utters words, draws sheepish visions that the world is mythic. Our fears, mystic.

The conquest of my spiritual chase is a big haired lady, queen of desperation, who pines, even forebodes of climes pleasant only to god.

Utters, "*god's the epileptic metaphor, autistic too!*"

Makes no sense?

It means what it says.
Nothing more.
Nothing less.

-----JDM

DIARY ENTRY #29

At least this so called war wakes us up, awakens the collective human consciousness. Pokes at the walking dead. We only define ourselves by what we own. Seems more like it owns us. We are sleep walking. Then, a war inspires us, makes us think, wakes us up! But, does it?

These are the times that try men's souls. War is hell, but freedom lost is worse. But, society needs to be afflicted in its comfort. Sad, but it's true. Without human disasters we would walk blindly off of cliffs. With pipers leading the way for us rats!

Like in this city, I see how diversity in people is really a strength. Our differences make us strongest. When will we wake up seeing this? Am I the only one who sees this? Or, are there other young people who yell this at the tops of their lungs only to be silenced?

And, if we all see it one day how long will it last? USSR vs.USA: no balls to light the nukes. So, we fight it out in Nam? Our memories are so short, so routine, so predictable. Our bellies selfish. Give of yourself you really give. My music was my gift. My gift to others.

Viet Nam kills, but it is only a symbol for other wars, all wars fought in our past, to be fought in our future, all wars being fought now. It is the very same war each time we fight, just under the guise of a different name. It does not matter the name of the war. War is war. Same 'ol shit! Just another day.

Wars may kill but the war raging inside us kills us most. It's better to be dead than to be alive and be a non-thinking, non-feeling robot. Who wants to be a damn automaton?

War is hell on the home front, though rumors circulate it'll soon end.

The real war is inside us, and it is just beginning!

----JDM

DIARY ENTRY #30

197--?

Think I'm going insane. Feel my mental powers fading day by day. I just break down and cry. So worried, so scary.

Torment. Suffer. Torture. Words to describe my insides. Pressures build up inside my head. Feel like it'll explode. More and more I can do less and less. Life's a chore. Just to get out of bed's impossible.

Thin line between madness and genius? I'm in the middle then, closer to madness, though. Can't take it. Put it out of my head. Voices talk to me. They come from inside, not outside me. But, what will the day be like when I can't tell where they're really from? Will that be the day I've lost my mind? Scares the hell out of me. Some chick friend, Lizzie, says, "quit the sauce, no more shit." Hmmm.

Gone skitzo, gone fishing. Plan to keep it only to myself. Don't tell anyone anything. Through our long talks we get close, talk more of thoughts, seldom feelings. So, I'm safe for now.

Went down to the red light district some nights ago. Chicks behind glass in fish bowls all for sale. Always wondered if anonymous sex was best? Or, is love the recipe for the best sex? One or the other? So, I look around, rent a body. They're all over, all around you, dark shadows looking over your shoulder. We stare into the night. See no one's faces, only eyes. My shadow side of darkness blazes brightly!

Dozens of glass booths line the streets with red lights inside. Secret rooms inside, too. Only false names spoken.

Watch out! What you see ain't always what you get. Behind door #3 they're really men masquerading as women. Shock of a life time for some. Funnier than hell for me watching Navy dudes absolutely freak out! Come running out nude....freaking!

Finally found *a she* who harbored bells on her doors. A ring on each finger. We loved by the hour. Kissed beneath a ticking clock. She coulda had a time card! Her tentacles though touched me. Glad no one here legislates morality, 'cause I'dhave missed out on her, cheating the desires of the libido.

Noticed in her eyes the poetry of these streets, the longing of her struggle to find love. She whispers how she can make my life happy, rich, fulfill my dreams. I whisper back, "not my life you mean, yours." She jumps back at the point of quiver as if I screamed that in her ear.

Love was not made. Only sex was given, pure pleasure with no inhibitions in the way. Unlike when you love someone. No strings = no love. Now, I've had both. Love and pure sex! Both love and sex have their curses, have their cures. One's not better than the other. Just sometimes you get what you need when you need it. That's all. As simple at that.

Legalized prostitution and legalized drugs lets you love as you wish, feel as you want. 'Cause some hypocritical government says, no? You can not do what you want with your own body? Bullshit! Legalize it all everywhere! Light up!

They did that all here. And, it's amazing! It rid the streets of disease and crime. Emptied the churches! No more mafias selling sex and drugs underground. Streets are safer. Have the whores get a license and insist they're clean. Blood test 'em each week for VD. And, cities can make TONS of tax money off it too. We got it and get it anyways. So, why even try to stop it? Prohibition never worked. Remember Al Capone? Seems the stupid rule the world!

'Cept, morality must dictate our laws? Wish we could get beyond good and evil, concepts only for the lame and lemming-like herds. They must have a hold onto security Pathetic! Man, if we ain't legalizing drugs soon the crime will get so out of control! You'll be able to get it on playgrounds. Kids with guns shooting in schools! It's my body, my life, let me do what I want with my own life! Who is someone else, some city official, some church to tell me what to do, think or believe?

Same difference with booze. It's the same as hash! Politicians have to protect their own jobs by repaying favors to the alcohol factories. Can't legalize hash since it would only create competition for alcohol companies. Give me a break. Pretty clear to see. We're not some blind mice!

No drugs! They say it's for our own safety! Each year booze kills as many soldiers killed in Viet Nam so far. No one gives a shit. But, on the war they freak out? Seems the real war should be waged on those who are stupid and drive all tanked up.

Do what you want but be safe! No one need kill themselves or others on their way up to a high. Take a bus, a cab, a streetcar. Stop controlling us!

Talk a lot of these ideas here in Amsterdam with Americans and Europeans. That's what we do all day. Debate these ideas. Talk it over. Which is cool! Lots of cool peeps here. Liking them, too. So open-minded and free here. Don't feel boxed in ever. Everybody's gotta come here. See it. Live it. Might be the only time in their life they'll ever feel totally free. I mean I've seen the future and it looks like this! I found a piece of myself here, too, but fear I'll leave a piece of myself behind when I leave.

---------JDM

DIARY ENTRY #31

Shit! They killed Vincent, too! Anyone who's too sensitive won't be able to take this world's, so called *reality* for long. That's why they all die so young! Lambs in the midst of wolves easily die of desolation, a slow form of loneliness, madness. Just exactly like the lost soul of Van Gogh!

So, he cut off a small piece of his ear lobe and gave it to a waitress. That is so damn crazy? They drove him to do it. The world is what drove him crazy. Couldn't take it any longer as he walked these same streets I walk upon, here in Amsterdam. But, it was too late for him! Worlds were never meant for that kind, our kind!

Bunch of us went to the place they got almost all his works of art in. Wish it was in Amsterdam. They say one day soon....I'd go everyday. Had to go all over hell to get to Appeldorn. Got lost in the many countryside's he painted. Saw the same field he shot himself in.

Looking at his art in this museum you begin to see his passion. You see he painted on backs of chairs, bottles, bottoms of chairs, soles of shoes, doors and windows. That is not madness. That is passion! His passion exploded onto canvas. Like mine did on stage.

But, my passion was only a show. Drama unleashed. They never knew it. Only knew the character they wanted me to be. I acted for them all. I did act my ass off. Like in some Greek tragedy they watched a drama unfold in my shows. Did they miss it?

Then, they confused what I did on stage with who I was as a person, who I am inside. The real me was lost up there while singing to them. Which was cool. But, I'm really not who they think I was. That's why no one recognizes me ever. They never see the real me. I refused to let them see....to let them suck my bone's marrow dry. I gave forth in my poems, my songs. If they wish to find me, find me there!

Resemble myself then little compared to now. The great Sophocles alive and doing well in LA, on stage, actor extraordinaire. Relocated to Amsterdam! Give me a buzz!

The times made me. I hardly made the times. Big world, cruel world out there. Like Vincent, I needed to escape it too. I ran as it almost swallowed me whole. Just a human but they made me their god, some hero, somehow. Can only fall off the pedestal then. And, as soon as they give you life they kill you. As with the Jesus!

With our little group, my little gang, we talked of our lives on the car ride back to Amsterdam. All marveled at Van Gogh's art. He only painted ten years but what an explosion of time! We were taken with his art but I was more taken with his life. His lust for life, the zeal, his intensity. His strength of passion!

Can't believe he was not happy. He had to be happy in those paintings. Like I was in my music. I was happy. So was he. We just grew tired of the world attacking us. Don't want to die like him though, check out like that. So, then, I'll just disappear into a crowd----great and total privacy there! The more people around you the easier to hide. Why I love the big cities so much!

Walking around I was your royal highness, drunk all night. I tripped over my feet on the street. Bicycled into a canal when we got back into town. Soaked, cold, almost drowned. Love these hineys here, those smooth beers pour. Wound up in a few cafes Vinnie frequented. Lots of Vincents in there even today, in the world today!

Painters, thinkers, writers, travelers. Art is not useless. Brings us out of the cave, makes us believe in our own souls, shows us we're more than mere beasts.

Talked with some Vincents at the café about art. 'Cause someone don't like what you create don't mean it ain't art. Just means you don't like it. Whose to define what art is? Say what art is or isn't? Shit, someone will censor the, DAVID and put a diaper on him lest you get a peak. God forbid! Beware of censors and the moral majorities of the world. Their only aim is to steal the artist's breath! Stop 'em!

I said just let people create what they want. If you don't like it don't look. Why is that so hard? Who am I to stop it? Anyone to stop a work of art in progress? All in the name of religion or morality? Whose morality? Whose religion?

Religion is only social control. We all agreed don't let them take our freedom away from us. Finally headed home then. Looked into the sky. Thought of stars. Saw the black of darkness for the first time here. So black a color like Van Gogh's crows, his last painting. His last look into his inner world.

Oh, played chess tonight too. Busted their asses. They got no strategy these punks. Got mine. All mine!

Reading again, *The Art of War*. Just love ancient Chinese thinkers! Got some inspiration. And, heard a whisper from a painter from a hell of a long time ago speaking to me, still speaking to the world. No one ever really dies if they live in art!

Spending lots of time with this group, this groupie cult of sorts. Got my beard back, black turban on, tell 'em I'm Nostradamus, they laugh. Some believe. Met him on Atlantis before it sunk. Some eat it up! Funny, but pathetic.

Knowledge is power. You give up your brain anyone can control you. Talk about exercising the mind a lot. Those games of chess and guessing first lines of poems help. Feel like a guru lately. Liking it, too. If Plato taught Aristotle and Aristotle Alexander, then for sure I've inherited all their genius. Then, I'm the greatest teacher of all time. Feel needed here! Useful! Respected!

No one wants to lead. Only want to follow. Could form a cult and lead them to their deaths, their minds so weak. Why do people allow themselves to become so vulnerable? Pity them.

Try to teach them. But, they want their decisions made for them. No wonder why governments are so strong who enslave these junkies with drugs and sex. Pacify their lusts with an Amsterdam and you're their hero. World needs heroes, needs more gods? 2000 years and no new gods? I'm their, *Lord Jim*. Only fragile egos demand followers. Only weak egos seek out leaders. Oh, you know it's funny as hell. You meet so damn many dudes and chicks here, so many that have met you already. So it's impossible to remember their names. And, I'm so bad at names. Some chick pops up, then says, "hi ya Jimmy baby." Damned if I know her name. Or, some dude yells, "Jimbo, let's meet for a toke." I feel stupid, look dumb, not knowing their god damn names. So, I say to him, "hey, yeah, let's do it......you're the dude in that band, right?" He says, "yupper." I'm saved. I say to her, "hey love, you're that beauty writing that book, isn't that what you said when we first met?" She's so impressed I remember. Shit, if I remember! Their names, their faces, nothing! Much less them. But, EVERYONE I meet is either writing a book or's in a band. Or, was in a band or wants to be in one. And, they ALL want to write a book. Say they're writing one. So, my ass's saved by the bell. Major relief for what've proved to be a rather embarrassing situation. Just hate like hell to be rude! It's funny as hell, though! Who isn't in a band or not writing a book? No one! I'll always use this if I get into any more binds! Always works! Well, these peep's talks, ideas, pleasure and company is all so cool.

City's great, too! Hash sweet. Booze's so endless. The state of the union is strong!

"If beauty is likened to a moment,
life is as a second in time.

The universe lasting twice a man's life."

-------JDM

DIARY ENTRY #32

AmsterDAMN!!!
197---2? 3?

Long for those warm ocean breezes, long to smell the sea's salt. I cut my finger to taste the ocean's salt in my blood. Desire it, now. Desire cool blue swells, white caps, sun warming a sand too hot to touch, too hot to walk upon.

Sat by one of Amsterdam's many canals. Longing, looking south.

Book of Poe's poems left on the cement ledge, at the canal, under some bridge. Miss it. Envisioned his many images, heard his inner plight speak so loudly to me, so clearly.

Nevermore. No ravens, near. All his words too, writ in blood.

For sure, poets are the unacknowledged legislators of the world!

Each day with the sun's rising creative spirits are born anew. Each dusk, with the sun's setting, upon the moon, they all reflect. Write. Envision a better world!

We wait in wonder of how they'll change the world.

------JDM

DIARY ENTRY #33

Medieval ideas-----irrational thought.

Life, the testing ground for reason.
Love, a state of bliss, utopia unrequited.

Incense fades, intentions rise.

The times which try men's souls is now:

"...the heart's sing.
Across the ages, bliss.

Every day, it rains.
Few, will come to bloom.

My breath, stops.
Heart pounds.
Eyes marvel.

Amazing how beauty came to be.
Came to be in you..."

-----JDM

DIARY ENTRY #34

Finally!

Made it home! Two days on the run. Ran for my life. Ran against the gauntlet of fanaticism. Fight or flight? I took to fight!

My little gang talked me into singing with a band, so, I did. One BIG ASS mistake! I mean, I like the dudes, so I wanted the chance for them to know me and me to know them. So, I decided I would sing for them. But, I did not want them to know me that deeply!

Yet, my music's me. I'm my music. I can't think of any other way to express myself. But, shit, this was way too much.

If in war the first casualty is truth, I lied to protect my identity as I physically fought against them. And, this was war!

First, I stood on a make shift stage, worn out carpet below me, empty keys on a dried out piano beside me. First, a poem or two. Some sang alongside me. Not too bad, either.

Old crates steadied speakers so huge-ass upon that I thought they'd crush. A few times they fell off and onto the crowd of a few hundred. Some kind of a warehouse, more like a whore house as free love and mind altering chemicals enthralled all late into the night.

Others also came onto the stage. Sang besides me, but, mainly, they only tried. Once in a blue moon you'd get someone good. They loved the Doobies! Only covers were sung. Stones. The Airplane. Rock n' roll ruled, was resurrected beyond the height of gods. I wanted to sing so badly inside. I ached. They kept yelling for me to. They cheered me on. "Go on! Come on!" I only had my poems! Wanted to, dare I expose my flesh again? A riot would linger in any note sung. I wasn't sure!

Inside me that conflict over and over, "do it. Do it!" This little voice saying, "come on, Jimmy, do it, do it!" Hearing it louder over and over. My breathing deepening. My voice not as loud as the feedback which pierced their ears. I read my poems again. Spit out from memory where they had been burned into my mind. My insides quivered. I began to hyperventilate, sweat, shake. Raging hard-on. I could not hold back any longer.

Then, the sons of bitches began to boo and laugh at my words. I SCREAMED into the microphone! Only too glad to pierce their ears with pain! Finally, I laughed. I yelled, *"I am the lizard king! I can do anything!"*

Silence pervaded the pathetic crowd. "So you wanna see it? Wanna?" Grabbed my crotch. Unzipped my pants, let it stand out! They cheered! They wanted it more than I did. Their empty spirits needed a charge of passion. From me! A jump start from my soul to theirs!

The band playing some soft blues, now. A hum, soft drums. A crescendo once in a while as I taunted the crowd. Their wills in my hand. Their souls in my pocket.

"Are you ready?" I asked again, "are you ready?" They screamed back at me, a jubilant, "we are ready!" The beat of the drum, on and on and on...bum, bum. Bum, bum, bum, bum, bum, bum.

Their music narrating me. Spellbound were the masses. I spoke, they answered. An orgy of pure rebel rock and roll! Poems ran into minutes. Time which must have been hours, until my voice soared, *"TOUCH ME....Come on, come on, come on and touch me babe! Can't you see that I am not afraid?"*

The band followed suit, another cover to them. A freeing of me. I let go! Like the release of an orgasm, my blood penetrated their hearts, stabbed at their wounds.

I sang! My body moved and conquered each moment in that windowless hole of a dive! No lights! Not even electric, 'cept for the stage. My electricity, the magic of the moment!

"With me you can do anything!"

Fragrant sweet smoke floated in the air. Hot whiskey burned my throat, gentle Jack stopping my heart with each swallow. I sang and sang and sang as mesmerized clans followed my every word. They were prisoners held at bay. In the silence they began to suspect,

"Lord Jim?"

I could not just read poems and be safe? No, I had to sing. Only sang to be free. My hair soaked. Lighters flickering in the air above a thousand heads. Into the crowd, red hots glowed in view, as their vices smoked 'em!

"What's going on?

We gotta fight to be free!

Make love not war!

Restrict our liberty to protect it?"

They cheered, yelled back, just listened,

"kill the evil thing!"

So infamous and dark was my voice that it cracked, leading them to explore their deepest senses. I'd fallen but they'd risen up. Took them to new heights when someone yelled,

"Hey, it's Morrison!"

And, soon, it all began! The powers of hell were unleashed as they stampeded the stage. Knocking down the keys and crates, wooden bins, the speakers toppled. They charged me! I could not move, like in a dream! Just stood there, pissed, touting,

"Come and get me you god-damn bastards!"

The band running for their lives, me directly behind them! They luring their prey! Some fucking riot. Something struck 'em all of a sudden. Reality's a heavy thing when you finally grasp it. Even heroes bleed.

I ran fast, faster, yet, in every corner, every alley, there was one, two, a dozen of them. Coming in at me. Turn around, more. On the side, even more. Up above, some too! Coming in to roast a fallen hero, now alive. Gotta get the fuck out of here. And, fast! Think someone snapped a photo or two. Flash in my eyes, blinded.

I could run but could not hide. Closing in on me. Cornered. Trapped. Cops now? Thought I just heard the siren's song! I ran so fast I broke the laws of gravity. But, what the hell! I'd broken so many laws in my life! As the angry mob moved in, all I could think of was her, that she may not have loved me after all. She was more afraid of being alone. Shit! Was that true?

Hard-on raging in my pants! My temples pulsating with boiling blood. I felt heat and tingles all over my body. My hair on end going through my clothes. Goose bumps too, even chills. I felt all my body's sensations all at once.

I kicked in a door, ducked in, and leaned against it. Heard their voices and footsteps run by. I hid. My heart racing. How would I ever explain to my capturers, "me?" I was an imposter? Yes, that was it. An imposter! Impersonator of sorts. Paid by the record companies to start rumors to raise record sales! Like John Lennon did with the faking of Paul McCartney's death for the Beatles.

All I could hear was my breathing and beating heart when someone spoke. Someone at the top of the stairs. "Come up here." Some bald street punk, big beard, tall too. Medusa's male counterpart, I thought. Ugly as hell!

Dutch accent. Intelligent. He knew of these street gangs and said, "prop this stick up against the doors. Now, come on up." And, I did, relieved. Spiders, scorpions, snakes, his huge eye looking at them through me.

Black widows. Some yellow and black, oh, something poisonous, weird beaded lizard.

He worked for some importer of foods on the docks. Fringe benefit for him was all the creatures he could carry home. All in glass jars, tanks, all heated, some with lights over them. Actually, it was quite surrealistic inside. Very cool, too.

I was most fascinated by the black widow, the most perfect smooth color of black and a red hour glass upon its back. Bold and bright red, redder than my blood. Absolutely brilliant!

"She spins her web, then, makes love to her mate then kills him. She's the only one of the two that is deadly," he softly spoke. I began, "human love's the same way." We both laughed. Friends for life. The tension was now gone.

Talked for a while. Smoked some from a handmade pipe of Italian marble he carved. I dozed and slept for a while. A day I'd say. He said he knew who I was. Read it in the papers. Told him not to believe any of their hype! *Problems occur when you believe the hyperbole about yourself.* Then, told him that I was thrilled that his paper called me, *Rasputin, the mad monk of rock n' roll.* This way I would never die!

He told me that only one very small drop from any one of these creatures could send me back to the earth. He cleared his throat, "some, like me, just want to live on the threshold of mortality and immortality at the same time."

I asked him, "really?" He nodded.

Snake around his neck, spider on his arm, scorpion in his hand. Calmly, I fell asleep again.

He believed in the cycle of nature like some believed in god. Said it's all a process of becoming, this life and death. I liked him. Admired his struggle, his quest to know, a lot.

When I felt it was safe to leave, he said he saw it in the news. How I died and he thought at the time he knew I was still alive. Knew that I would never die.

Amidst good-byes he kept saying, "I know where you are." I said, "now I am going to have to kill you." He had this shrill of a laugh. Kind of freaky.

Said my secret was safe with him and that he respected my right to live life as I chose. That all people had that right. I could only agree.

"Good-bye, *Tod Hunter*, fugitive on the run," his last words to me. I was relieved, more amused. Did he not really know who I was?

He may have gotten my name, but, I never got his. Think I saw it on the door buzzer on the way out. The name, *Gordian Knott*. So, he was, *Gordy*? Cool!

I was finally home alone with my freedom. Was this the omen of how things were soon to be? Wild chases? Near misses? If so, free me from my freedom. For I am only running in a prison of my own creation.

All I could think of was that little box, and what my "contact" would do to me if I lost it. I found a completely sealed box, big as a pack of cigarettes, in my pocket. Major relief! Soon, I was to traverse to Budapest and its drop off at a Turkish bath. Only wondering what the hell was inside it!

Needed to get the hell out of this big, small town. On the morning train, I would leave.

I'd soon make my escape from god-damn, Amsterdam!

Damn!

------JDM

DIARY ENTRY #35

Venice-----here's where my Nefertiti had wished to honeymoon!

Today, St. Mark's Square was flooded. Good though, cleaned off all the pigeon shit.

Kind of gloomy, misty. A gentle fog rolled in. Sure could smell the sea. Not much up for writing lately. Not much to say. My memory's clouded over, in a daze. Feel down, poems never flow anymore. My muse, gone. Had I forsaken her, abandoned the mind spring of my inspiration? The dry fountain.... Amazing, I can write now.

Sit on the square and drink coffee a lot. Think. Watch people. They watch me. Watch birds! More interesting and much smarter than people, often.

Lost, dizzy, looking for my hotel room. Canals all look the same. This city's a maze, some damn floating prison. Exiled here, you're trapped forever. Who needs prison bars then?

Send me to prison? Miami's on my mind again. For what? And, how is it that the so called, "*freest*" nation on earth, America, has the most people in prisons of any other nation in the world? Anyways, I'm doing my time here. Cold and alone. Eat anchovies on crusty breads, wash it down with bottles of cheap wine. Isolation is prison in the strictest sense.

Met some guy, said he killed a man in self defense. Over beer and some slut! Said he had more freedom in jail. There, he didn't need a job. Free food. Said this so called freedom out here was the real prison. I gave him some money, said, "it's all in your state of mind. We create our own prisons and at the same time hold the key."

113

Here, you talk to a lot of people. One talk in ten means something, is worth anything. Quite the difference from Amsterdam. My time's all I got these days. So, visit an art gallery a day. Look at a few pieces each visit, learn about a dead artist or two. Call it a day.

Saw the Tinteretto painting, *The General Pope*. Pope Julius II. Once, popes led armies and crusades. Killed in the name of god. Wasn't that long ago, either. Popes put on armor and fought, even owned this very land I sit upon. I looked into the eyes of this painting. This pope was hell bent on war, a real killing machine. His eyes stared back.

Art is a mirror, plainly showing us ourselves. Defining who we are. But, few fail to realize that life imitates art. Imitates even general popes on canvas. Seems I can say so little of this out loud or to others. I must place sensitivity over truth. Better to lie or to hide the truth than to hurt someone's feelings. I think that this is just beginning and think it'll really fester and the day will come when we'll all be paranoid to speak our minds. Talk about mind control, then!

Even an artist's work will be suppressed, our words censored. Brave new world of thought police will lurk behind every corner. Beware! But, afterall, it's only life, and, life is just the aberration of time.

Fell asleep? Not sure the day, the hour, the year. Dingy in here, damp and musty too. Some hotel! Dark, can hardly write. Have I died and gone to hell? Looks like the perfect place for an opium eater to die. I just wanna live. Live my life. I'll never be alive again, never was alive before. Curious to explore everything I can. Learn all I can. After all, the unexamined life is not worth living.

I've captured the universe here in words, looking into this very moment of my life for all eternity. Why was I born when I was? From all the millions of sperm that one made me? Ain't got the answers. Sure got a lot of questions. Need my personal pocket Buddha to give me some wise ass answers. Hope too in Karma to render to me some good I've begotten.

If I'll never live again can I at least experience my own death? Feel sorry for those with miserable poor hungry lives. With problems of evil and no answers. Why evil with an all loving god? Dump the god and an answer appears: evil is just a realm of life, pure random acts. Life's absurdity. For, where did the god come from? Where'd he get all the materials to create this whole universe? How'd he know how to create it? Who says that god is even a "he?" Oh, what was this god doing before he created all this? Creating a hell for me? Love the heat, turn it up baby!

Humid here, canals stink like shit, but, the wines sure are good. People friendly. Feel alone, though. Isolated. Liking it but missing------- missing my Eve here in the garden of Eden.

-----JDM

DIARY ENTRY #36

Restaurant on the Amolfi coast.
Somewhere in Italy. Some year, some date, unknown.

Mozart's Requiem. The funeral mass he never completed. He died writing it. It plays on the radio. Never before had I been so deeply touched by music. Not even by my own. To sing the blues right you have to live the blues. To live the classical, one only listen to their heart. Classical's heart is the music foundation to all great music.

The depth this music brings me to within myself is like none other. Never knew I could feel….. Can't seem to put into words, not sure what I feel. Here in Italy, hear mostly opera. It is in their soups, their wines, their hillsides, even in their kisses. Prefer it here in Pompeii to Milan or Naples.

Something always getting stolen in Naples. Tires off the car. Shoes on my feet. Laugh one minute cry the next. Guilt by association, don't look into their eyes. They'll see your weakness and steal more than your things. They'll take your soul, too.

Rented a hot Alfa Romeo. Cherry red! It's almost erotic. Like with beautiful women this car has fine sleek lines too! So, I soared with her along the Amolfi coast. High cliffs, blue seas, way, way down there. Gulls and imaginations soar. Never seen such beauty. Perfect time to die. Even more of a perfect place to experience it.

The Amolfi coast, where the catch of the day is always good. Where bright flowers bloom, and glazed tiles, hand-made floors glow under your feet everywhere you walk.

Feel compatible with myself, lately. Especially, here. Miss no one. I like my own company. Don't think much. Just stare, look out onto the world at the edge of the sea. Sometimes, I can observe myself from above myself. Zombie like trance. Automatic pilot. A gift from god? Some god, any god, my god? This beauty I feel, this wonder I seek, is beyond words. I can't describe my deepest feelings in words. Can't really explain this at all. My heart lies too deep for words.

Take these day trips, pick up hitchhikers. Back packers along the way. If they look dull to me or might bore me, I tell them I'm Italian and don't *comprehendo* English. And just don't pick 'em up. It sure has worked a lot, lately.

Feel like some butterfly of the opera. Some gypsy kids played some Hungarian folk tunes on their violins. Gave them some Italian money, Lira. Two million Lira equals about a dime. Feel like the Rockefellers. Better to give to them then to have it taken from you. Why make them into thieves? You're happy, they're happy, and you keep them honest.

The viola pierced me deeply as the gypsies played, me throwing piles of paper cash into their hats and violin cases. One asks me, "you like rock?" I tell them, *"I am the rock!"* Tell them, *"think of rock as my father and me as his only begotten son."* They laugh. I like their decadence. Their dirty minds, their evil intents. They stink, too. But, they keep me thinking, keep me alive.

I drove them to a nearby town. Time to fleece a new place? Some play the music, others do the pick pocketing. They linger by the car window, smoking. Staring at me as I leave. Seductive in those dark eyes. "Hell, we're not even gypsies," they swear. A noble profession, I think. They sing, you dance. Frauds, yes, but, they are what they are. No hidden pretences.

Most live quiet lives of desperation never knowing who they are. Much less what they are not. Those are the ones, not just in Italy, but, all over the world, who dance in a pathetic solitude. We see them all over the society. Better to know you are trash then to try to disguise it with a tuxedo. Either way, you still stink.

Give me my musicians any day. Have to meet their kind in Budapest, deliver the box. He said, "you don't ever want to know what's inside." It tears at me, though. For, I do wish to know. A Turkish bath. Sounds cool. Do I need a knife between my teeth and a long mustache to get in?

Shit, I don't need any more excitement, but, promised the dude this favor. I'll make it good. The night still may be young now, but, tomorrow, it's Pompeii where the old never age. The dead never die.

Miss my long talks, good for shit chats. Miss hearing English spoken as I seem to find less and less Americans around lately.

Here, they all talk so god-damn fast. Staccato. Opera. Must be the thick coffees they drink winding them up?

Hell if I know where I'll drift to next. Maybe, Morocco? Or, Rio? Live like a hedonist everyday. Just drifting off alone, just a drifter of the universe. The stars, my road map.

The silence in my head speaks louder and louder with each passing second. Can hardly take it, already.

On nights like these my only friend is my wine. It never leaves me dry, nor alone.

-----JDM

DIARY ENTRY #37

The blond beast inside my existential crisis hemorrhages!

I descend into the depths.
Gaze into the abyss which stares
back at me, screams:

"Come to me this time, and, this time, do.
Your breeze, elusive.
Your spirit, evades.

Once, in the mirror,
a phantom.

And, in that moment, a dream.

To be,
to be as true.

To be as true,
but only with you."

------JDM

DIARY ENTRY #38

At night, the pain comes. In my right hand often, I felt a searing, intense burning pain.....

Can't wait 'til she comes. Pacing, and walking the floor. Can't wait 'til she leaves. Want her gone, outta here. Alley slut! Give her some money, she gives you the world. At orgasm, the beauty dies at peak. The more intense the feel, the greater the fall, the shorter the feel seems. At that moment of ecstasy, life is timeless. No thoughts can enter your mind or invade you. The intensity thrills.

I think that the orgasm is replacing the cross these days. A much better god. A much greater feel to this moby dick.

No music pervades my spirit these days. No movies. No news, radio, TV. Mojo the hermit, I long for peace, quiet, simplicity. The tranquil life. Just me and myself. I am longing for the remembrance to time's past.

I listen to my mind speaking inside me. Won't stop. Can't shut if off.....on and on! Keeps me awake all night. Wonder if that voice inside my head is really me? A consciousness? A soul. It speaks, I listen. Speaking to me is the will of some god?

Then, let MY will be done! Rather trade the climax for the cross!

Me, the mad monk of rock n' roll. Rasputin, just re-invented.

-----JDM

DIARY ENTRY #39

*Strawberry fields...nothing is real. Strawberry fields forever....*the music plays. Man's will to power? No atheists in foxholes? <u>Bullshit!!</u> I look right into the mouth of this bitch and laugh at its face.

To climb to her rim, thousands of feet up, only to meet a Coca Cola machine? See Pompeii down below. I'm looking down into the graveyard of civilization.

The greatest of social controls over the masses is superstition. Give this volcano a name and you've created a god. You found a way to control people through religion.

LIGHT MY FIRE! VESUVIUS!

Killer of thousands in their luxury town homes below. Human bodies, dogs, crawling people all encased in volcanic ash. Like concrete statues one sees their faces of death, screams you hear even today through them.

They all lived life and lived life very well. Never thought they'd die until she blew.

But, the real ruins are their lives as the testaments of their living is their frozen-like corpses in stone; just as they died. In the very spot.

No one believes in their own death. Don't feel even at the top of this volcano I'd ever flow downward, What lives   dies. Not so bad to die. Only bad to live life and only exist. All existence and no essence is pathetic. Only to be a part of the machine, a spoke in the wheel, that is life?

We live, we die. Down below they died over 2000 years ago. Then, what will our legacy be 2000 years from now? Only our death? Like them?

I prefer to be knows as, **the rock and roll poet**. A poet who tried to change the world, leave it better, make it beautiful. No one can survive their own death. Only the businesses called churches say there is an immortality. Only the weak believe it. The churches grow richer. Build more cathedrals to rake in even more money. The vicious cycle, like history, repeats itself over and over.... The casualty? Our wills!

I look out across the roof of the world. I touch the clouds. Soar where angels fear to tread. I look around me in a circle at the world below. I command its future. I am the superman who can out think them all. In my words, my songs, I make them think.

THINK!

Open your minds! Use your imaginations!

Like Warhol's art, I gotta shock 'em outta their complacency, the boredom they call life. Then, they will listen, then they will see. All art must shock. All music is art. All human tragedy possesses a birth, if for only a moment, wakes us up. Like volcanoes blowing their tops! That wakes us up!

The human condition is to survive. Humanity exists for all to live passionately, walk humbly, think and love deeply. Mere survival is for the herd, the sheep, the animals.

The ruins here at Pompeii is where we rise up. Wake up. See what matters to us in life so we can pursue it. Live it! They died so we can live. We live so others can die having truly lived. But, how many will? Or, for how long?

My life is a ruin, my music in ruins, too. Seldom, anyone hears my message. Never am I recognized for my true poetic worth.

Like one big toilet our lives spiral down the cesspool to a bottomless pit we can't survive. Like being buried alive in hot ash. Don't want a life of quiet desperation. Don't want to be a piece of history. Don't want to live in the past or be a museum relic.

Fear the walk into the gentle good night if you have not lived.

Only regret what I <u>didn't</u> do in life. Never on a death bed has someone regretted what they did. So, let me do it ALL! Pour ash, hot lava, tar on me when I'm dead. Not when I am alive.

Ruins make me reflect. Wake me up from my stupor of ignorance and folly. With them, I find an answer to life, hear the question, "*why die having not lived?*"

The crater in this magnificent living volcano still rumbles! I hear thunder, hear Vesuvius saying, *"you too are next!"*

Let's only live, for no one gets outta here alive!

-----JDM

DIARY ENTRY #40

From the very bottom of Italy's boot, across the waters towards Greece, I stare up into the sky and wonder. Look up. Dream. Think up.

On a mission under the stars. They guide me, steer my fate.

On the ferry from Italy to Greece, across the Mediterranean. I feel like Shelly and Bryon on their way to war. Their romance to save the Greeks, hail the Agamemnon of so long ago. Evening came so early, tonight.

I imagine I can see the fingers of Greece across the dark sea. Stars still shining, my heart still dreaming.

-----JDM

DIARY ENTRY #41

The garden's a grave, really.

If love is a breeding ground, flowers live only off the dead.
Humus. Waste. Bone.

Be not afraid. I go before you....

In my father's house are many mansions. I go to prepare one for you.

Flowers at the gate. Butler at the door. Three into one.

"...dance, the soul does.
Moments for more, I long.

Once, a you.
Now, no more.

How I long, shed tears,
wait upon dawn.

Come once more to you..."

------JDM

DIARY ENTRY #42

Truth or consequences. Truth or dare. Now or never. Never say, *never*.

They just want their tunes. Listening to the Dead. Ripped tie dyes. Their Jerry wails on. Funky sandals, long braids. Heavenly hash drifts into space. Music, like all great art proves we're human, separated from the beast.

Off by a camp fire with some drifters looking down on Athens, sleeping near them inside the Acropolis. Ancient grasses grow underneath me. Flowers of evil bloom. Descendants of the same plants the ancient philosopher Socrates walked upon?

Someone, maybe a "pop-philosopher" strums her guitar, hums songs of non-violence, angry songs against the war. Hungry, I eat some goat, taste more curry, though.

Under these temple ruins I watch her, intently. She seems to cry as she lazily plays the guitar. Playing homage to the temple queen, Athena? Supple body, sumptuous skin, Athena lures me to herself, her beauty, through the music.

Life is more difficult for an ugly woman opposed to an ugly man. She keeps on singing. Her voice like that of a butterfly which stings like a bee. Like the sirens she attracts her lovers by her voice. It's her only way. In her eyes I felt her fear, for no lovers buzz her way. We all listen, in our own way, to this flower child of peace.

Peaceful here. Induced states…. Mellow.

All in our own little world, together. Like everyone else in the world.
------JDM

126

DIARY ENTRY #43

Death be not proud in an ancient Greek cemetery. Immortality lasts only a generation. Little pieces of bone washed away by rains shine in the sun at my feet. Old graves reopened for new ones. Stars hover above me. I look up and see her eyes

watching me, my Rose. I wonder as I wander......

On tomb stones I see crosses as well as images of ancient pagan gods. Seems all men must kill the father to be the son. We're just spirits in a material world, why life's so impossible for us spiritual people.

Visited Plato's Academy today. Hard to find----no ruins, no tourists, no signs. Only a garbage dump, a real land fill now where Plato, Aristotle and Socrates walked and taught. The same academy Aristotle left heading off to tutor Alexander the Great. So, I sit nearby civilization's first university. Now, just tombstones amidst the dead. Within this dump!

When I am finally gone hope they put confederate flags upon my grave. Proof, I was a generation's voice of rebellion. Hope they remember me unlike those who have forgotten their dead buried here.

These graves tell a story. Someone dead a year has a lot of flowers. Dead five years, fewer. Ten years, one or two. Twenty five years dead, once in a while you find a flower. Thirty years, nothing. They're forgotten, totally. New sections of the cemetery fly flags, flowers beam under sapphire skies. The old section, you hardly see anything at all. Ancient section, just an archaeological dig. Our mortal lives are longer than our immortal lives.

To be aware or to not be aware.....our bones await the dust, our skulls fade into the dirt. As if our minds never existed.

-------JDM

DIARY ENTRY #44

Tried to stand exactly where Socrates died. But now there's a Mc Donald's over it. Give them the hemlock under the golden arches!

City stinks. Athens, polluted as hell, noisy as sin. Congested, I've got a roaring headache. Explore the city by day, escape it each night.

Olympia, the home of the Olympics. Found out that athletes back then had to compose and recite poetry, too. And, they played their games naked! VERY cool! Count me in!

Sometimes, when I think that religion is the opiate of the people, I have to say that maybe sports is. Just as base.

Travel the road of least resistance, most do. I'm just trying to keep off that dead end.

-----JDM

DIARY ENTRY #45

In the stars, her eyes...

My senses allude me. I wonder if the things I see, the things I hear, all that I experience, is reality or just an illusion?

Bugs crawl on me at night. I awaken, they're gone. Someone calls my name. I see no one. Someone follows me. I look, no one. Someone follows me now. Think of that captain, that private sailor in the Greek isles. Can't seem to forget his story and that evil eye which follows me now. I'm the man who knew too much. Hearing the bugs crawling inside my skull, gnawing at my brains. The demons inside me stir up, rise up, confront me. My fall from grace. I can only remember his tale, the murder he committed.

Glee in his eye as he laughed hideously. "Watch out for him," his first mate told me,
"he's the devil incarnate!"

Some flashing lights, crude words, loud insults. Over some beer in the hand of some girl, some Helen. A chance of do or die. He literally beat his opponent to death, bare handed, double fisted. Outside a bar in the Greek isles.

Then, this captain orders his crew to carry the dead crew man, take him back to the dead man's own boat and dump him in the aft cabin. Then, they continue to party all night long. Drinking the dead guy's booze, smoking his hash until they all pass out, tossing the bottles out to sea, the pipes into it, too. All drinking an evil's witch's brew.

When they awaken the next evening, hung-over, they sail his boat past the deepest tide. Then, they tie the anchor to the guy's foot and throw him in. Mere, fish food.

They all laugh in relief, high fives, some tribalized male grunts. Tether his boat back to the dock and move on. Looking for their next ship to captain and sail. No one ever knows of the murder. The victim disappears into the depths of the sea. Never met a murderer until him.

Salty looking beard, black teeth, ragged clothes. Scared me to death just looking at him. Still does. That captain took me to the isle, ran some tours out to the famed birthplace of Apollo. Picked me up a few days later as I indulged on the nude beach.

He follows me now. I hear the camel nearby, stir. He comes for me? Like some demented Captain Hook, he wants to tie my foot to an anchor? I awaken in a sweat, realize my imaginations gotten the best of me again.

He has no need, no reason to follow me, I tell myself. No water for him to command here in this desert in Macedonia. Yet, I know his secret, his first mate shaking in his need to tell me, tell anyone, to get it off his chest. Soon a mutiny on the bounty!

And, I look up into the sky, into the stars, and see her eyes. Eros and the goddess of chaos rule each night, spin the orbs. From all the stars, all that chaos, I find constellations. My consolation. Chaos to constellation. I seek to find the familiar even in the heavens.

When I recognize the North Star, a planet, a constellation, I feel peace. Mankind, from evolution's start was wired to make chaos into constellation. To create the "known." The cave men did it, so, we do it too. Superstition was invented.

The bull, the fishes, the rams, the astrologers created them, putting the lines in between the dots, those being the stars. Might like to sail under the Southern Cross. Across rough seas, gale force winds. I will go. Will go to visit a constellation I have never seen in this hemisphere. Romantic, the idea of a Southern hemisphere. A whole new place!

Then, while on my boat there, I'd look up, notice nothing I recognize in the Southern hemisphere. Fear would turn to creation as I'd begin to connect the dots. Like with clouds, making pictures from the stars. To feel safe, I'd make my own symbols to smile down upon me. Chaos to constellation. Like ancient man. A new astrology.

Be it north or south. East or west. Still recognize her eyes in the stars. My Rose. My comfort against the night.

-----JDM

DIARY ENTRY #46

Seriously searching Bacchus!

Long to drink from Dionysus'
never empty chalice,
stir in a drunken stupor,
sleep amidst the Elysian fields,
make love with the vestal virgins,
dance with the satyrs!

Leaving Greece with all the sentiments my heart holds, craving to know
that master alchemist who designed my mind.

-----JDM

DIARY ENTRY #47

Passion.
Something, someone's inside my head…..

[FRAGMENT MISSING]

To whoever reads this, transcend me. Once an option. Now, never a possibility.

Can't take these nights, their laws, ups, downs…..the US and their prisons.
Such a philistine place!

Love is a delicately danced ballet. All dancers playing their parts.
I'm not afraid of dying. I'm afraid of having not lived.

[FRAGMENT MISSING]

Awaken dreamers from your slumbers!
The world had not changed. On stage, only I had.
Sonic intoxication.

[FRAGMENT MISSING]

Students, be greater than your teacher! Be better than me.
Lucy in the Sky with Diamonds look down upon me, now!

-----JDM

DIARY ENTRY #48

[FRAGMENT]
Alone. Alone with all my thoughts.
And, memories.

Just thinking of all of them alone,
by myself.

------JDM

DIARY ENTRY #49

[FRAGMENT]

Curl up with my bottle of wine. The warmer the taste, the better I feel.

Do I drink because I am unhappy? Or, am I unhappy because I drink?

My sweet companions, wine and sleep. Hold them both, longing for more.

[FRAGMENT MISSING]

-----JDM

DIARY ENTRY #50

Like my wine, I often wonder of her, smell the roses.

[FRAGMENT MISSING]

Did she love me 'cause she needed me? Or, need me because she loved me?

-----JDM

DIARY ENTRY #51

[FRAGMENT]
(Severe water damage)

……make it in the day, the world…..

……without you…..

------JDM

DIARY ENTRY #52

He follows me with a glance. Gazing, peering at me from this way, than that. Inside my head I wonder of him, his shadow which looms over me against night's walls.

Seems when you know certain truths about life, you alienate most everyone from around you. Family. Friends. But, I choose not to be like my family or friends. I think differently then them. So, I am alone. My fate.

What say you? Say you are free? Not slaves anymore? Slaves to the dust, yes. But, not to tyrants or old ideas, ancient ideologies? You still are unless you eradicate such non-sense from your heads. If not, then be a slave!

To flee, run and hide. Like from him. He's the lowest. My father, myself! The caste system of the military I despised and rejected. Reject now. No, <u>DESPISE</u> now! I wish not to be like him. I'd rather drop acid than bombs. Perfect hits. My leap of faith!

Kent State. College massacre. All but forgotten? The blood of students, unarmed, zooms around in my head like a bug stuck on sticky fly paper. Free speech? Right! Their voices once loud, now silent. Most have nothing to have their speech protected from! Then, they MUST change that!

Tyrants fear more your ideas than your speech! Get off your asses and think! Follow not your fathers. Rebel! Rise up! Think for yourself. Let not your leaders think for you! The will to power is peace unmasked. Afterall, we shall overcome. Then, let us!

Over my shoulder, under my neck, he looks. I almost shudder when I look away. I fear not this valley of death though I walk alone. For, those who rise up are with me.

Are you?

My cup overflows!

-----JDM

DIARY ENTRY #53

The ancient kingdom of Pella welcomes me. In ruins, rubble can still attest to Alexander's empire, his father Phillip's desire for his son to be the greatest.

Alexander's tomb lies near? Archaeologists and native diggers show me where his father rests, and, his father and his father. Like dust upon the moon, I walk back onto a history few remember. Macedonian kings abound in memories of these royal graves. No one knows who is buried where any longer. A pathetic legacy, but how then can I expect anything better?

Follow not your fathers!
Kill your fathers!
Like Alexander lead your own way!
Direct your own destiny!

As gnostics we fulfill our own dreams, conquer our own lands, embrace any path we choose!

"Alexander, Alexander!" I yell, "my hero rests here?" I've followed in your bloody sandals. Life may end as yours did, but, is not hopeless without a god. God is only hopeless without a man. We have great heroes like you, people who were actually once alive to look toward. Gods are made in the image of men, and women! With weak clay feet.

Like orbs in the sky above, they direct my course.
Stay the night.
Light my way, Alexander!

Even at break of day I see so many beautiful stars and planets. I can smell smoke from the diggers small camp fires. Coffee brews. Their day of digs yet to begin.

Though it is so cold now, it does not feel so. I'm warmed by my ambitions, warmed by my desire to be where he had once been, once walked.

Alexander looks down upon me now. I wish upon the dawn for me to be as great as he once was. Still is.

-----JDM

DIARY ENTRY #54

Fall, 197----
Budapest train station

Some kind of a one-eyed drifter! The type with a knife, the blade between his teeth. Turkish prison escapee, one can easily see. Long black beard, stray smells, gruff voice. Always angry.

Traversed the hills of Bulgaria, Romania, Transylvania, to find the castle of Count Dracula. This experience I can not even begin to talk about......yet! But, I must document it in these very diaries. Too much happened there. Just for now, it's unspeakable....soon, soon.

But, Budapest, I am here, city staring right at me. My mystery box in pocket, giving me the jitters. Paprika on all their foods, hot anger inside the firmaments of all their Hungarian bones.

The journey here seems like a blur. I remember so little. Actually, all of life seems to be one big blur. Lived, traveled through communes, some disguised as cults seeking utopia. Found more abuse of this ideal than the real thing, though. Wonder of all I have missed. Even wonder just how I got here!

Crossing the bridge from Pest into Buda, I found the bath house right away. Built into the mountain's base. Just as I was told. Got out the box. Ready for the drop off. That pirate's still eyeing me, minus the eye. Just a patch but no parrot.

So, I go into the place. Kama Sutra stuffed into my back pocket. A real Turkish bath, alright. Belly dance music playing. Belly dancers swaying! Steam everywhere, only see through a fog. Many foreign tongues spoken. Mumbling, a gibberish. Some humming a tune.

Seediness makes a man paranoid, and in here I seem to be the only one tense.

Relaxation eludes me most, fearing for my life. In a corner a man whispers in the dark, "come here, yes you!" Is this my contact? I've protected this box for weeks. Its traveled alongside me like a friend for a thousand miles. I am not about to give this to just anyone now.

I was told I'd know who was to get this. Though, how? I fear for my life with the pirate near or looking over my shoulder. I am afraid when I see him, but more afraid when I don't see him.

Now, the adrenaline rush in my head makes me fear these moments even more.

Lost in this underground cavern, tomb, this labyrinth of caves, the moisture drips and drips and drips.....my feet splash with each step I take. This fog still encompasses me, still rolls in. Can't even see my hands. Once in a while it'd break and I'd see tiled floors, Turkish mosaic walls.

From behind me, all of a sudden, I felt a cold knife blade on my throat! My neck slit? My life flashed before me----again! This time for good? I waited. Hardly breathing. Hardly heard a sound, much less making one. Then, suddenly, I felt the box being removed ever so gently from my hand. I reached to grab it when I felt a pierce into my hand, soon hearing the knife fall from the palm of my hand. The box, gone.

The crimson tide poured, sounding like some waterfall. My hand hurt but fear encompassed memory as I reached for my throat, afraid to swallow. A hand grabbed my neck and I lunged at it. To get away. No luck. I was pushed into the wall, frisked, feeling the small box still in my hand!

A silver blade came near me. From the pirate, reflecting deep the blade's color into my eye. But, it was not my pirate. It was a woman! A scarf over her nose and mouth, her face under some long sweeping beret or drape.

As my life fled before me, I dropped the box, it sounded like a ton of bricks bouncing. Her eyes now in rage, widened, ready to bludgeon me, she fell to my feet. Dead!

What the hell was going on?

My pirate now appearing, laughing, "so, you see, you need me too, even if I'm not as pretty as her."

He killed her before she could kill me!

He spoke again, "she's not your contact!"

Then, who was? Him? Out of the shadow a man's hand was extended to me. I could not shake it, right hand bleeding and deeply cut, deeply pained. A whole right through the palm of my hand!

Someone else it seemed had picked up the box from the floor. When it fell. This shadow of a man thanked me and said the pirate was my protector since Greece. So, I was not mad then? Was not hallucinating?

He asked, "you been paid?" I responded, "adventure enough was ample pay!" I never did see his face.

My left hand was wrapped in a gauze by some mysterious force. For, I recall nothing. Then, I woke up in the bath house. I find it is days later. Proof of 100 didn't even melt the bottle? My head sore, my hand not hurting. Felt it was some dream.

Surrealistic memories danced before me. Asked at the entrance of a pirate, some dead woman, a force of men. His turban shook as he said, "no, no, no women please," laughing at me, his teeth rotting or gone. He kind of looked like the pirate!

So, was it real or just some dream? Lost in a drunken stupor, tripping out from some absinthe or mushrooms?

And, then, I found out that I held the box. But, it seemed like I always had it. Had it even still. But, even that seemed unclear now. My few days here, the parts I remember were too much to remember. Wanted out real quick.

Caught the train in the center of town. The woman at the ticket counter kind of looked like the woman who assaulted me in the bath house. When I took my change she glanced into my eyes with that same look of rage. I knew I had seen her before. Or, had I?

It was then that I noticed that my hand was no longer wounded. Neither hand was. She seemed to chuckle at me as I kept staring at the coins in my right hand.

It seemed that I could not separate reality from fantasy. But, that was always how life was, right? Was this life real or all but a dream? Ironic, I was headed to Prague. Heard the Soviet soldiers there were rough. I feared them not. Shit, had been through much worse, much more.

I really looked forward to Prague. City of Kafka, master of illusion, where in the metamorphosis of life we emerged from our chrysalis.

Asking, are we all but actors wandering about in someone else's phantasm, someone else's dream?

-----JDM

DIARY ENTRY #55

Resurrection's, canceled!
Subscription's, granted!

Within love, the wish is to find not someone who
transforms you into a new person,
but, leads you to yourself!
"...the world dies each time someone enters death.

Their world, gone.
My world, yet to live.

Life, the dance.
The dream nature's always held.

Reality or myth?
Some wonder.

Especially, me..."

------JDM

DIARY ENTRY #56

".....would you fear the Rose's beauty though its thorns pierce you...?"

I think of her, no....<u>dwell</u> on her. The music's never to be over!

The planet venus so brightly shining, so low in the sky. It looks down upon me as I write. As if it was all mine.

I wish upon the night for me to one day be all hers. Or, is it out of reach? Have I only loved to taint her with a scarlet letter? Are people that strange?

She could have been anyone I suppose, 'cept the one I wanted her to be. Can't change her. Or, recreate her.

Only, accept her....?

-----JDM

DIARY ENTRY #57

Visited Auschwitz on the way here. Too much pain. Too many Soviet soldiers. There, a superman vs. sub-human? Seems that's what it was all about. The most blatant abuse of intellect and hatred. 6,000,000 dead. May it never happen again. But, it will. So much we know, so little we understand as our little planet drifts off towards Andromeda.

In the camp only life mattered as the wills of the living increased each day. But, day by day more died then lived. Must one almost lose life to recognize its value?

For, peace is always easiest in the abstract----hardest to get along with your neighbor. But, that's where it starts, one by one, if not, we all die one by one.

Sit upon these same streets again. Eating, feeding cheese to the many dogs, bread to the many pigeons. Think of love, of her. Smell the fragrances and scents from the Parisian flower market. Can't help but think of Rose.

Want to tell her, want to say, *I really wasn't that way. I was only acting the part.* When you are cast as a villain you begin to steal. Rock star, you rock. Sure, took many casualties along the way. Yes, even her.

I've changed. I'm different now. Cleansed, washed in the blood of my travels. But, she won't believe it. She only sees the lies, not my love. 'Cause my love doesn't resemble hers she sees an empty heart in me?

Show me who you love and I'll show you who you want to be. I call out to her. I want her to transform me, save me, rescue me with her love.

Will she speak to me, spit at me, even remember me? My face so rough,

149

so coarse from my journeys. But, the real travel has been the journey into myself. To find me. To discover who I really am and who I really want to be. Can't she see that?

I was curious my whole life. Did not want to die curious. Wanted to see it all, live it all. Why was that so wrong?

Should I bring her some flowers, a single red rose? Tap on the door? Cry in her arms?

There are two kinds of love, two kinds of lovers. In love, one is the lover, the true lover, the main lover. The other is the one loved. This one loves less. This all began with Eve's power over Adam. This is why love seems so impossible to create, much less maintain.

Eve loved Adam more, he loved her less. Lopsidedness of love, the imbalance of hearts in a war. How can love ever balance? Then, will there ever be true love? Happening just once in human history? The cosmos explode at such a rare event?

We create who we want the other to be. Not find who the other really is. I want to tell her this, show her that it's just not about me anymore!

Love is more than just mere body worship. More than just a cult of beauty.

But, will she listen? For, it's the truth. And, truth is always stranger than fiction. After all, life imitates art. Not the other way around.

------JDM

DIARY ENTRY #58

Patmos. St. Helena. Botany Bay. Elba. Cyprus.

Like strings of fire, their guitars burn as they play. Enthralled, I devour it, dream of Spanish moss hanging, me below the trees.

I'm ahead of my time. Mis-understood, too. The battle rages on. Not on the outside, but, on the inside. Face it, life for most is nothing more than high school with money. But, for some of us it is much more. A battle, a fight just to stay alive as thinking and feeling human beings!

My consciousness battles my unconsciousness. The life I'm aware of wants to live. Yet, when in moments of an induced state, my unconscious self only wishes to die. To over-dose, jump off a balcony. Never feel like this when I'm sober. Only, when bombed. Not even aware of this, only told by others that I tried to do this, do that.

My inner being just may win out one day?

Some three years since my so called, death. I return to the city of lights where that all "began." Am I going nowhere fast? Going in circles 'round and 'round. Where I'll stop no one knows? Life always comes full circle, history always repeats itself. Pray, not Miami. Now, they'd lock me up forever for my so called crime of, 'show and tell.'

Lock me up, caged in, bars between their world and mine? I would rather die. That's justice? One day something is illegal, the next day it is not? Wish only to keep my freedom and never find 're-discovery' back into their world. Though, I do long to travel to the states again.....if I've changed will it all look different?

Long to lay on a confederate battlefield, looking across to the graveyard where my ancestors lie, fighting for the stars and bars. Flag rustling in the wind. Inside, I'm torn. Wrestling over.....

There's always something about my life which tortures me. For, it's easy for me to live in my music, my art, but, never my life.

Like Cassandra of the ancient Greek myth, I too speak the truth. And, no one believes my words. And, I didn't do it! Guilty as charged in Miami? I'm some so called criminal for the expression of art? Meager music on stage?

Is so called criminal behavior immoral? I'm immoral but not criminal? And, morals are relative, trendy, right? And, they change like the fashions of the day. One man's hero is another man's villain. But, will they ever hear my truth? Ever recognize art?

Want to dance to the bright horns of these Spanish blues. My port wine flows. Even tequilas, pour! Want to dance, serenade the Andalusian queens. The bongos sooth my restless spirit. Paris, home to a little bit of Spain. I love this bar where their boiling bloods warm my passions. The singing of passionate words I don't understand, but I do feel, moves me into their songs. I can't but help sway to the beat.

My diary here in the dark soon guiding me back to her? She'll soon see I'm complex, not complicated! She'll take me in, yet!

For, if Rose won't take me back there'll be no meaning left in life. And, if life holds no promise, I wish to fade as the sun, disappear as the nova.

Drift alone out to my deserted isle.

-------JDM

DIARY ENTRY #59

Music chose me. I did not choose music.

Like Lennon and McCartney meeting for the very first time at the grave of Eleanor Rigby. It's all fate, meant to be. Pure destiny.

At the, *Whiskey Go Go*, I worked my ass off to be a star. Now, my star fades and I am all too glad. But, they won't let me die. Like a wooden puppet they've made me their god.

The music will never die and that's what I wanted. Let me die though, but, never my music.

From the brawl my eye's kind of closed, left side of my face puffy and bruised. Hurts like hell. But, only when I breathe. She felt sorry for me. Opened the door. Opened her heart. In her eyes she let me back in. It was tearful, and, so I proposed. Want to leave the continent, Mexico our destination. Trek to the Maya pyramids, bike with the crystal skull in my back-pack.

She accepted! New bride, new baby on the way. Days of loving were more than just scx. She's irregular and I'm to be a dad? Hope it's a boy. In love, we all play our roles.

Told her I didn't want to be called Jim again. Wanted this to be my new life, my new identity. A totally new existence. No need for the gideons, got my own personal Zen now!

Like medieval monks who changed their names as they embraced a holy life, I want to be called, *The Apollo*. Brilliant. Beautiful. Braun. She insists she will only call me, *Polo*. We laugh.

Try to tell her that Carravagio, the Renaissance painter, took a new name as he pledged his life to being an artist. He also took a vow! He was simply called, "**M.**"

She giggles, rolls her eyes. Says I am not Carravagio. It's funny and I am happy. But, it's true. She sleeps with me, in my arms. I can't help but think of all the possible worlds, all the possible lovers in the universe, and it's come down to just us? Count out billions for just this one heart? She brings me to my romantic self, always did. Bring her flowers, single red roses, always.

She begs to know my stories of hijacked trucks in Bulgaria and our gang using pure morphine for weeks. Local hospitals in a dizzy. Confessions of an opium eater!

Did the years take me to Egypt, China, Ethiopia, the Andes? Did I find my dreams? Visit lost tribes in the Amazon? I invent stories, names and places when it's convenient for her to travel with me.

India, Arabia, Japan, "The Far East," she wonders did I sell tea, trade arms, sell slaves? If it didn't all happen, as I tell it, it should have. Could have at least.

Her gazing eyes take it all in. And, to think it all began in this apartment. With her, my new life, my new found freedom. I'll tell her all about my travels, even my secrets.....

Her flat looks different to me, as if she's re-arranged something. Not sure what though.

Still want to burn my poems, these diaries, my songs and little sketches when we get to Mexico. One big, *auto de fe*. All burned at the pyramid at Uxmal to the god of magic. An offering of myself in the name of Apollo, at the temple of these gods. Want to be liberated from the pen once and for all.

Oh, she actually snores when asleep. Sometimes, I can't help holding her nose until she wakes up. Makes me curious this noise she makes.

Still unsettled about tomorrow night, kind of nervous, more worried. Overwhelmed to hear their music again. My music, again. The Doors back in Paris. She'll be with me.

It's all about the noble struggle, all about music. The mother of my birth once sat in that audience. She reached towards me, I pulled back. My mother, myself? Now, in their audience will they pull me in?

I feel old, older than ever before. Though, I may look young...looks are only a deception. Even as I grow older I try to hold onto my youth. I won't let it go. If I do I'll grow old all at once and die. Like Dorian Grey.

Die, die, die. No, no, no.

-----JDM

DIARY ENTRY #60

Camus. Mann, Hesse and Sartre. Searching for a dude named, Godot, and reading voraciously these days.

Rose works on giving up her apartment, her things. Only so much we can take to Mexico, she says. Fewer books? We have stacks of my books to take already. I don't need clothes, only books, I tell her.

Speaking of books, I wish to soon transfer her diary into this one of mine. Wish to read of me. Wish to know all she said, all she thought of me while I was traveling. Wish to read of me. She can never know I wish to know her thoughts on me. But, I just gotta know. Killing me....

We plan to get married in the next day or two. Finishing up paperwork. A plain civil service. I need a new name for the French passport to get me outta here. That'll make me a bigamist, then? Rose and Pam. Could easily be a Mormon. Like a prophet, their sultan with casts of thousands. All those harems of wives. A different concubine. One for every day of the year! Give me that planet now!

I'm soon to get a new name, a new passport, and, a new wife.

-----JDM

DIARY ENTRY #61

Gave her a long kiss! First thing I said when I came up for air was, "I'm glad my kid's not going to be a bastard." Us, the new parents to be, with no money, hardly even a name. Until I gave her the box. It had to be broken into to be opened. Made of wood from cedars of Lebanon. Some ivory, some carvings. Tribal designs.

I helped her open the box. Inside, we dazzled at a small bag of about a dozen one carat Burmese rubies. Bright red, perfect specimens! There must be a god after all! My wedding gift to her! With this box, I be-wed.....widened eyes, halted breaths, and many more kisses!

Since there was no wedding cake, the ones as high as hell, I did not need a shotgun. Shoot the target on top. Some funky fountain or a miniature wedding couple in black and white. No wonder why people get drunk at their own weddings. Ours was simple: jeans and t-shirts.

She needed the money, as did I. So, we traded the rubies, all 'cept one, for cash. I am not to sure where or when I got them, but, she loved them. 'Bout as much as I love her.

----JDM

DIARY ENTRY #62

Such a beautiful place! Makes one fall in love with death. We strolled through the place on our last night in Paris, my wish. All the great writers, greatest painters, stars of the stage, most brilliant singers, rested here. Too bad they're all dead. NO more great people alive these days! She says, "no, not true." I say, "yes."

Rose and I walk past my grave. From a distance a very large crowd gathers. What do they seek? True, we all seek. I sought to make love to Rose there weeks ago in hopes of conceiving my first born child. Upon my own grave. She finally agreeing to it.

We walk, talk, her and I hand in hand. Anxious to leave Europe. Seek a more exotic life. Longing for the sun, a bright tropical sun, blue skies, vast jungles. This time tomorrow we'll be in the Yucatan. In Mexico!

The headstones looked like chairs, and, for the first time I noticed that there were names on the those stones. Real lives, real deaths.

It comes that god-damn distinguished thing, *death*. We all do it, comes to us all. It's like poetry, a different time, a different line for each one of us. And, we're not even dead until a funeral, a state, someone alive declares us dead. Certifies it! Insane!

Hamlet said it in a better way, "*to be or not to be*." That is the question.

To be, the answer! The reflections of my life!

Like waiting for the sun! Soon to be the concert.

-----JDM

158

DIARY ENTRY #63

My Last Night in Paris
19 - -

They tried to tie me to my music career by getting me to bite on that, "big golden apple." Sell my soul for fame, money, respect. But, if I agreed, music would soar but so too would midnight strike. Couldn't bite that rotten apple. Loved my music too much for that.

I was making music, not fame, nor prestige or money. The rest of the band didn't see it that way. They never did. Never will. After all, I was a poet and if I sold the music biz my soul I'd only have to do what they wanted. I was born for more than just mere happiness.

They offer you homes, cars, cash, hash.....the bait. Most nibble and then bite. Then, they've got you hooked. You never want the '*good life*' to end. So, you live in hell the rest of your short life, eventually dying. Just like Monroe, Hendrix, Joplin.

See, the stage was my high. But, I did my act over and over. Nothing was spontaneous. Rock 'n roll robot. Tried to be original, but, the hot shots said it wasn't 'safe.'

It seems to me that I was only original when I said the hell with them and read my poems, jeered the crowd, did MY own thing! If I finished a show leaving all shit-faced drunk, I knew I did my own thing. And, I had succeeded! For, then I had not sold out to the record industry. 'Cause the music was about me, only me, and not them!

Same shit as in the corporate world, this music world. Military world the same, too! I had to explain so much to Rose. She asked. She always listens, never interrupts, intent on knowing it all.

Pam couldn't listen for that long. Soon, she was a spinning top, off to a new boutique, a new bar, drinking a new drink, listening to some new band. Kissing some new boy.

But with Rose, even her eyes listen to you. I feel her holding onto my every word. She had become an instant audience, something I craved especially this day!

The clock finally struck, the hour had appeared, the night ultimately arrived. It was the DOORS first concert here in Paris since my death. It took some four years for them to return? What the hell was the hurry? They're still trying to show me up? Be one up on me? Prove to themselves that they're better than me? They want my fame! My legacy! They always did, though. Let them shoot for the moon. Cause they'll only get dust! No one will ever surpass a shooting star!

You don't need some fortune teller to know the band will do a few albums under my Doors name, that the records will be shit, that they'll break up. For, I was the band!

Then, they'll do this VERY SAME show over and over. Different city, same show. I never did that. Had something original every night. They pop out of a can, scripted, predictable and lousy! But, without me they always were nothing!

And, they're superficial and ungrateful. Never even visited my grave. Just left Paris after the concert. Never came by the grave to pay tribute to the reason for their being: me! My music! My vision! My genius! And, so, yes, it kind of hurts. But, fuck 'em!

So, I curse them. My spell: may their shows reek, their albums fail, reviews dog them, their band crash and burn! Big jet airliners need to come down to land, too!

But, I did try to listen to the band, objectively. I sat on some grass under the open air with Rose. Eiffel Tower in the distance all aglow. A mass of people all around me. Like they always were when it was me they came to see and hear.

The band yells, "Jim are you here?" The crowd chants, "Jim! Jim! Jim!" Someone next to me screams, "damn it, Jim, you here?" I jump to my feet, yelling, "I am! I'm here!"

Soon, I get booed. Told to sit down, get the fuck out of here. They yell at me even more, "fuck you! Get the hell going! You're crazy!" I hear it all. Feel little pain!

The band begins to play, Ray on keyboards. The crowd recognizes the song and everyone jumps to their feet in one big burst of energy! All, cheering! They light up, drink, dance, abandon me. Never felt more alone, more desolate. I try to make my way to the stage, but, I am quickly pushed back. "God-damn, let me up there! I'll give you one hell of a show...." Rose hangs onto me. Says I can't, I've changed, there's no turning back. You can never go home once you've been to Paris!

As the concert plays, I hear more of their music than mine. And, it's sick! Dull, sounds all the same. Soon, the fans are bored, restless. Soon, their music fades. My old songs, resurrected. The crowd once again, happy. I listen to the music, my music listening to me.

But, I don't remember hearing a sound as I sat back down. Just saw their faces. The fans, their mouths now moving to my lyrics. I want to scream, "wait, they're MY poems! My songs! Stop!" But, it's no use. I'm deaf, intoxicated by the crowd's frenzy. I can't move. I begin to weep. Hold Rose, close. I feel forgotten, just wishing that I was a dead legend. A living legend feels no glory. A dead legend feels no pain.

Only past memories, of past shows, are distant in my brain. I've faded from grace, from life. I'm a no one. A nobody just like these fans next to me. Perhaps that is why they come to listen? To feel like they are somebody?

Did they want to see the DOORS tonight, or, were they living out my dream through the memory of: *Jim Morrison?*

Yet, soon, I finally realize that they've declared me dead. I finally had their permission to die. To fade into the night. I could finally die in my fleshly life. Stamped death certificate and all. But, rise and enter into eternal life through my legend. It was finally consummated! I was finally immortal. A god. That shooting star!

Under the stars of an outdoor rock concert the faithful are absorbed, mesmerized into a musical ecstasy. Mystical sounds, sacred, stir within the frenzied baptism. The rock star: their priest. The amphitheater: their cathedral. The music: their religious rite. A new religion has been born! And, I am their god!

I felt completely defeated, yet, at the same time felt completely uplifted. My memory they've assimilated into a myth. While at the same time never repudiating me. I felt honored. Soon, the evening became bearable, the music enjoyable. I could finally hear it.

I told this to Rose, jammed into a little café after the show. She said maybe the band didn't visit my grave as they felt my spirit being was alive? They felt my legend so strongly that there could never have be a grave for such a great? Bullshit excuses! But, I was less saddened by her wisdom. Or, maybe I no longer cared? Gladdened by my victory? I didn't know.

She cares for me as a mother, and, is more than just my friend. Love, when it beckons, follow it, it may never return. Love always directs your course if it finds you worthy.

Soon, Mexico. Wish, Cuba. Wishing for a revolution!

-----JDM

DIARY ENTRY #64

Chained!
Victim to my own torture!

Leave!

Depart!

Go!

Even Zarathustra demands you flee
once you've found him, his truth!

Fodder disciples of your own.

Behold the man, speak:

"...so great a feel to touch life again!
To return to reality, the down turn.
Winds blow, ways thunder.

Freedom is found and then quickly lost.

Memories too, my friend.
Love lost, my foe..."

-----JDM

DIARY ENTRY #65

At 37,000 feet
Quite high

She's immensely intelligent, anyone can plainly see. Life's beaten her down, so. Is she my alter ego? She's the heart I often fail to find within myself? Her head rests upon my shoulder. Silently, she sleeps. She keeps me alive, young.

The way into someone's soul is through their vices. She has none, except me. She holds my soul in her warm tender hands. She keeps me breathing while my music is the life blood to my existence.

"...with her I have traveled into the heart...
Knowing my listening was not in vain,
and, my song not unheard....."

------JDM

Only like to fly when I'm asleep. That damn hum of the engines is like the sound outer space must make.

Beware of these mineral spirits, these drinks. They only amplify worldly time and exaggerate the importance of life. Make eternity a spiritual orgy.

Feel like some Brahman flying above the clouds, Kamasutra in hand.

------JDM

Where do we go from here? Always worrying about art and where it is headed. I mean, what's its future? We've seemed to have done it all. Expressionism, Cubism, Dadaism, Impressionism, one *'ism'* after another *'ism'*...

What the hell is next, then? No ism's left?

What do we create after everything's been done? 2, 3, 4 dimensional works? Mixed mediums? Robotic? Computer? How can any great artist ever rise up, stand up as someone new and original?

What we need more than ever is a renaissance where tragedies and myths give rise, give birth to a new art. Only in tragedy, war, conflicts, will a new art be born.

Are the skyscrapers art? This airplane art....is......

-----JDM

Jung said that modern man is mature at the age of 30. So, that is my 30th birthday gift? Maturity? My wisdom was always here, I can attest to that truth. I just needed to find ways to tap into it, access it.

Still want to copy her diary. Have to. Getting a new diary to copy it all down in. Read of me, under the tree, with bread......maybe some brandy.

Stewardess, make mine a triple.....

------JDM

DIARY ENTRY #66

The Anastasi might have disappeared, but, the Maya never did. We live with them on their very land. It's not just land, it's the sacred ground their ancestors lost their blood upon over countless generations.

She writes, stares at me. Writes in her diary. Stares at me. Writes some more. Come on, I gotta know about me! But, in her words. Can't take it no more. So, here we both write, often draw, paint, but mostly explore.

Spooked around inside some king's palaces. Visited caves and pyramids. I tell Rose, "shhhh....be quiet, hear that?" At that moment of silence I growl like a jaguar! She jumps out of her skin! I only laugh 'til I cry. She, too.

There's this local doctor we met here. He's a shaman, the local witch doctor. He rented us our little hacienda on his land. We're one house of many. Two yankees amongst many Maya around us. They don't speak Spanish. They are indians who still speak the old Maya tongue. They've not been corrupted by the west! Bravo!

The Maya always smile. Sometimes, I'll say to them in English, "hello you little fuck head," and, they smile, act happy, lost in their own little worlds. Funny as hell! Of course, Rose thinks it mean. What they don't know won't hurt them, I say. Plus, it's all done in good fun. And, 'fuck' in Maya means, "I like you." She won't believe me! Still, she laughs, which is good. I love being with her! I love it here! I love them!

The hacienda we rented had to be rebuilt, somewhat. Actually, had to be totally rebuilt. One big heap of sticks on the ground. Made us want to cry. Just burst out laughing looking at it! A real scream! HOLY SHIT!

So, we cut down some palm trees for a thatch roof. Put some tin over

166

that. Used sticks for the walls, put some boulders at its base, and some concrete stucco around the sides to stabilize it. Not bad looking, either. Kind of the way the Maya have done it for thousands of years.

It's really quite cozy. Blanket for a door. Safe and comfortable. One big room. Dirt floor but padded with a lot of blankets. No electric. Candles and oil lamps, a soft glow hums inside each night. We like it. I'm putting up some hammocks for us. Though, I love sleeping next to Rose on the floor. 'Roughing it.'

Brings back memories of when I was a boy....loved to sleep on the floor. Loved to camp, sleep in the tent in the backyard. Every noise in the dark being a monster.

Sometimes we sleep in the nearby king's palace when the snakes come into our hut at night. Don't bother me none, but, Rose can't take it. She screams and begs for that hammock. I laugh and take my time getting it up. Sometimes, I grab a snake and sleep with it. On my chest. They do calm down. They like the warmth. Like me.

We eat a lot of corn, maze they call it. They grind it, bake it. Corn bread, fruits, lots of fresh water nearby. We don't cook. Everyone brings us food all the time. They trying to kill us? So far we have not gotten sick. All we need with Rose and the baby on the way.

Tikal, Guatemala, Panama Canal, civil unrest. Chitenitza, Tulum, Chiapas. We've visited a lot of ruins, tombs, and ran from bullet fire more than once. In bullet fire even your ideals flee fast.

Banditos often come 'round at night. Upsets our village. Want food, liquor more. Always a bandana on their face, eyes down. They're harmless. I insist we give them all they want, lest they think we're harmless only making them harmful.

I've learned how to make a brew from the villagers. Better than moonshine. Some mash for a bash. We all love it. Banditos smell it. They come into our place. I show them the jug is empty. The real brew stews beneath, buried in the middle of the floor. All mine, too. Some Maya recipe I got from the old indian priest. Said they made it this way a very long time ago. Gets the job done. Strong, but has a bitter, dry taste! One hell of a kick!

I've collected a lot of artifacts, clay idols and jade gods. Buy them for a few pesos. Have this one in the shape of a severed head which was used for blood sacrifice. Frightening feel to it!

One artifact, some god, huge, holding a pot, is filled with hash now. The burning incense transports me to the heavens. I love to inhale, breathe it in, my clay feet transcending the ground.

Mail ordered some books about artifacts from Mexico City. Just drawing each artifact I discover, cataloguing and working on my own book of them.

Just returned. Muddy and dirty. Went to this ancient town, Coba, earlier today. It's in ruins. Was able to climb the pyramid. On the top I was a god, *the lord of the flies*. Could see the ends of the earth.

The Yucatan, my world now.

-----JDM

DIARY ENTRY #67

She's really pregnant. It really shows. Morning sickness. She feels better as day goes on. She feels better as she knows I want to settle down. Raise a family. Be only with her.

Many caves, nearby. Some with vast pools of water to swim, bathe in. *Cenote*, Maya call them. We go, often. Bats and soap accompany us. The locals won't. They see it as the home of the gods. Worry for their safety. Not us.

In a rain forest on a hot humid day these caverns make us feel like gods. I always take a book down here so I can draw and write about what I see. Sketch these artifacts down here. We never touch 'em. They fit the place. Some I've drawn and painted with natural pigments, using berries, leafs and clay. My collection is now vast, close to 1000. Vases, jades, beads. I wear a necklace with the rain god, *Chac Mul*. The people won't look into my eyes any more, won't talk to me. Some believe I am, *Chac Mul*.

I've created an altar for worshiping these deities, an altar to worship myself. The Maya peer out their windows, reverent, but still afraid of my sacrificial rites.

I insist on blood for my altar. For my practices. Blood from beasts, they provide me. I place the blood in these ancient bowls their ancestors once used. But, once used with human blood. Wish I had it too.

Though we do not speak the same language, they understand clearly my role as their priest. At night, the men often sit, drink, smoke a Maya phallus pipe of peyote. Stare into the fire in the center of the village.

One man speaks, telling some legend, they are all hypnotized, even terrorized by his words. You hear the night move here in a jungle. In this rain forest wild jaguars, prowl.

We see visions as we stare into the fire. We point into the flames saying what we feel, what we see. It's ominous this world. Often, I sing, recant poems of mine, mythic stories. They listen. Their dark eyes light up in horror as they wonder of this gringo and why fate led him to them.

They tell me about something. Something evil. Something hideous. Something lurking out there! Something that they can not speak of. Some boy who once lived in Merida, a boy who knows some words of English, tells me they wish to take me to that place, a cave, "tomorrow, tomorrow night." This jungle boy, Mah Kina, says, "but, only at night, though." Why? He won't answer.

The boy says they will not speak about this any more. But, it is about, "*the sign.*" The sign, some moment in time their shaman foretold long ago? I agree to go. Want to go right now. The fire is low, and, Mah Kina says they say we have miles to go before we sleep. That, we must sleep first. I nod in agreement.

A temple. A cave. A sign. I wish to find mine, too.

-----JDM

DIARY ENTRY #68

A sacbe, the Maya word for road, led us here. We simply followed it. Climbed up to the top of this pyramid---the one they say a tiny magician built in one night. When we looked out onto the rain forest we saw the darkness in the distance making its way toward us.

Montezuma's revenge?

The sky looks alive. Half day. Half night. A calm in the air, the smell of rain,

lingering. It was a tropical storm for sure, maybe even a hurricane. Had the persona, the face and might of Zeus!

"Father, it is your son, Apollo! Spare us," I shouted out over the rolling clouds! Rose urged me to get inside the little temple at the pyramid's top. It just started pouring, winds soaring. Lightening flashing. It's the end of the world! We should be so lucky! I told Rose, "2012 in the Maya calendar is the year the world ends!"

I wanted to look out at the storm but Rose would not let me. I won't turn to a pillar of salt should I look? So, we sat and watched the light show. Blinded by the great thunder bolts of lightening, sent down by the gods, down by Zeus, for his son. The storm, mighty as Cortez, rages on. In it, I hear my destiny.

-----JDM

DIARY ENTRY #69

Days after the storm, water still stands everywhere! Long snakes and banana spiders at our feet, seeking dry lands. Creepy to Rose, not to me.

Got the roof fixed just now. Kind of damp in here. Got the lantern burning on high. Nice heat! Sleep on the floor with the snakes. Not Rose, she's always on top. Loves the hammock.

No late night fires, lately. Everything is so wet. Still want to venture out of this world and into the next.

Down into the cave....

----JDM

DIARY ENTRY #70

Pam loved me for I was Morrison. Rose, 'cause I was Jim. But, without either of them I could not be great, much less be who I am. Last night I dreamt of them both, both with me here. Us all making love, loving life together!

I keep reading the, *Popul Voh*, the Maya bible. I keep feeling the top of my head. Dreamt that I grew two horns. I feel some protrusions on the two ends of my head. It's strange. Can I will myself to be the devil?

Radio doesn't work anymore. Ruined by the storm. Keep thinking how the radio was something out of this world for them. How I once sang one of my songs to them which was on the radio at the time. These Maya loved it. Trying to dry it out now.

Music was once my living, but, not my life. I have these people now and they need their priestly god. Me!

Now, night had finally fallen.

I wore the animal skins they gave me over my body. None of my own skin showed. Antlers, too. The shaman blessed me. I had become the creature, ½ man, ½ god. I recited some words of Zoraster, and, even to them it sounded sacred.

They were afraid to enter the cave, this tomb. But, how had I waited for this moment. Finally, after a week of waiting the waters subsided. I could be lowered down. Looking up at them I remember their beautiful smiles and kind eyes. Pure colored skin. I felt dizzy from some potion they fed me.

Temptation breeds salvation, equals fascination. Why is it all religious rites, all cultures, wished to alter their perception? With wine, peyote…..beer….

Inside, it was hollow, an empty cave. Like a woman's womb. The tomb allowed me to walk on the human bones, skulls, and protruding rocks. Soon, my little lamp was over powered by the darkness. My eyes became more perceptive then. Spiritual powers overcame me. Blind, but I could see.

I chanted, drank more of the potion, feeling the animal skins growing into my body. I tried to rip the skins off me but they would not come off. They were now part of me, me part of them. As a tribal beast I danced and worshiped with the rites of magic their ancient ancestors used in a quest to find their essences.

After what seemed like hours, I was drawn to a large clay like pot crawling away from me. I pulled at it. It would not give. Only crawling deeper and deeper, away. Fast, too. Finally, I touched the pot, recited some priestly chants from the Vedas and easily pulled it out from the cavern's wall.

I bathed in the miraculous waters. Waterfalls still poured inside this lost sea. Along the underground river the waters flowed furiously and spoke to me. Saying, *"all of the earth is your Brother! All of nature your Sister!"*

Inside the pot, under its lid, I found a book. I recognized it though I had never seen it before. It stirred within me ancient memories. Inside, some codex, an ancient Maya manuscript wrapped in animal skins. Maya hieroglyphics painted in blood over resins on each page. Pages made of lamb skin. What did it say?

It was a thick book with glyphs, delicately painted pictures. In a former life I once could read them, now, it had faded away with re-births. I longed to know what the words said, what they meant. They seemed to speak to me.

Looking towards the pool I swam in moments ago, I saw a mermaid. She saw me. But, when I approached, she was gone. I was now naked. Indeed, this was a magical place, and, I would draw a map of its location. Come back to find her….

The strength of these little people was not enough to lift me back up to earth again. My furs had been shed. Lost, unable to be found. Was I still too heavy in my born again life? I held onto the ropes. Tightly, they pulled and I floated upward. Some kind of ascension. Book in my hand, I led them to the camp and they followed. Me, making a map of this place.

Around the fire, I held the sacred book that their eyes would dare not touch.

Together, we only wondered what it said, that which it proclaimed. Mah Kina, I must find him. I needed to know what the book would speak to me, what it might say to us. My manifest destiny!

Days later upon my return, map guiding the way, the mouth of the cave had been swallowed. The entrance of the womb was gone!

-----JDM

DIARY ENTRY #71

Mah Kina, the young Maya boy tells me the book is one of predictions and prophecies! Predictions and prophecies of the Maya people! But, it is written for all peoples. All time! All the world! This is an incredible find!

But, the boy trembled as he threw the book back into my hands, vowing never to touch it again.

Ever!

I only seek the prophecies they made. Need to know these predictions.

Mah Kina must help me!

I'll never rest, I've vowed, until the day he does!

-----JDM

DIARY ENTRY #72

Yucatan - Mexico
Hola!

Poverty = Crime.

Now, with the rains and floods come the hungry, the homeless. And, the stealing of food, crops, raw materials right off other's houses. My poppy plants gone, trampled upon.

Few share the little they have. Man by nature is selfish. Must learn how to share. Man, the most intelligent of beasts but greedy as baboons.

Mah Kina, nowhere to be found. I cry!

-----JDM

DIARY ENTRY #73

Radio's now playing!

If you can't be with the one you love, love the one you're with!

Kerosene lamps, kerosene cookers, filled. Damp outside, finally dry inside. Lately, we speak little. Lately, I see visions, dream dreams. She's distant. Says it's the obsession with the book. The grueling suppression of not being able to see myself in a mirror.

What more can be said of wives with kids?

The villagers avoid me, avoid the book.

An omen I was never to find? One question I have then! Just one! Why?

-----JDM

DIARY ENTRY #74

Date unknown.
The place unrecognizable.

Id, Ego, Superego = god the father, god the son, god the holy ghost.

On this *XTRA* radio station, in L.A. or here in Mexico, the wife of Jim Morrison, Pamela Courson, they say, is dead! Is this then <u>the</u> sign? She wrote saying that she'd give me a sign, a sign I'd recognize right away. A sign we would finally be together.

So, either she's dead? Or, is she?

-----JDM

D. J. said that she was some kind of a whore, drug addict. On the radio, over and over, they play my songs. Is this it? A sign from our lady?

-----JDM

Infuriates me, their fucking lying words! She was more than anything they ever imagined her to be! Only told Rose I need to leave for L.A. 'Family emergency!' Needed to go alone. Told her nothing more.

Will I find Pam dead or alive?

------JDM

Will Pam be in the way of Rose? Rose in the way of Pam? Inside, my body's shaking. My stomach's nervous and weak. My breathing, heavy.

Must go. Everyone's safe in this village. No danger.

Diary, my Maya manuscript, with the clothes on my back, some cash and a ruby, I head on out.

Needing to know. Needing my wife.

-----JDM

DIARY ENTRY #75

Sisyphus rolls up the rock. The mountain top, he stares down, aware of his fate for it to rock and roll. And, then, he to begin anew, never cutting the bonds with eternity.

"...wait, but not so long.

For what, I can't know.

Yet, over time, you'll fade.

From memory, from thought,
then, I'll be free.

Free to wait-----thinking on you,
but remembering not why... "

-----JDM

DIARY ENTRY #76

An anarchist who puts the rational animal the political being aside?
Then, a poet who says farewell to poetry is not such an oddity?

"...to sleep is to die.

Death, slips as night.
Quick as day.
One day, us all.

It seems untrue.

Yet, we'll never know in the dark
depth of it all, when.

That then will be death...."

-----JDM

DIARY ENTRY #77

Finally arrived! At LAX. Hate to sit at airports. I fidget. Planes fly. Too loud! Headache throbs. Can only wait for the crowds to clear on out. People board their planes. They all know it's me here? I hide, hailing the next cab. Or, just sleep here? Hard to write. Hard to think. Hard to know what to do next. I'll soon see.....what I see in the mirror is totally up to me. Right?

-----JDM

DIARY ENTRY #78

Love must be re-invented!
The roles of man and woman, redefined!
Artists must first become poets of revolt
lest our lives fill the graves, be covered
by the dirt.

"...long for beauty. Crave the past.
Once, a time, only coming to me.

Before me they dance.
Night only weeps.

Why life comes,
so suddenly we fade.

Mysteries we seek.
Memory, we harbor.

Drifting out to sea----
Wishing only to see---

your face..."

------JDM

DIARY ENTRY #79

California Bay Breezes!
1974

Constellation moves to chaos. I recognize nothing. Nothing recognizes me. Abandoned, forsaken, I feel like the son of god upon a wooden tree.

Santa Ana, hitched a ride up here. Then, got the Harley traded with a ruby. Destination, *Fairhaven Memorial Cemetery*. Where angels fear to tread?

Will I be able to recognize her? Will she even recognize me? My hair's white, almost gone. My face, aged. My voice deeper and harsh. My body, thin. My will, broken.

I wait. Knowing she never wished to be cremated. Sitting near the columbarium. Waiting for her. Know she's alive. It dawns on me, that's the god-damn sign!

Our love a funeral pyre? Never!

Still wish to surf Hawaiian seas, make love to an Aborigine down under, ride horses on the beach at Tahiti, laugh in Papua, New Guinea. Bali and Indonesian winds speak my name, call me near.

Wishing to be inaugurated as the new Narcissus, I stare at my feet walking upon the waters! Me, a new mythic sensation flying towards the sun! I want to see it all, live it all, be it all!

Those drunken Australian kola bars beg to party with me. New Zealand mountains await me on the ski slopes. I breathe Machu Picchu's thin air, feel its'cold, touch the Inca's gold. How ever do I crave the thought of traveling with her. So many places, so little time. She must be here, she must be alive!

And, man, I gotta know…..if knowledge is power, then I'm the one weak in my not knowing. And, I must know it all…..if I am to be among the supermen.

But, I don't see anyone I recognize on these rows of names. Kept reading them on the walls. Always told her, *"seek your own happiness, find your own bliss."* Had she? Had she even listened, ever heard me?

In the many names, I finally find hers. Found her name on that little door,

MORRISON
Pamela Susan
1946 - 1974

I clenched the Maya codex next to my heart for direction in my life. Keep wondering, do any of the predictions or prophecies speak of me? Tell of us?

Need something to unseal this little door with, break it open with. Must break into the other side.

Desperately seeking a screwdriver, a knife. I shake. My nerves rattle me.

But, I must unseal it. Soon, I'll remove that little door. See inside.

Need this time to think…to wait, calm down….hey, it's some funeral driving on by……in the distraction…..waiting to make my move….

I will open that little columbarium door, yet. I got to. It's do or die.

Inside, a little note of where to find her? Or, only an amphora full of ashes?

------JDM

Jane Doe Morrison by Travis Sykes

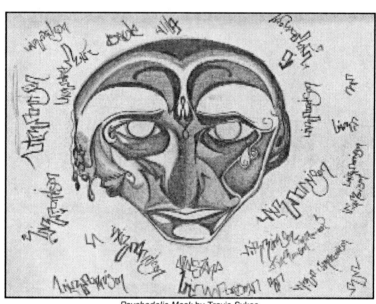

Psychedelic Mask by Travis Sykes

Poppi Plant by Travis Sykes

Evil by Travis Sykes

Very special thanks to:

Professor John W. Rooney Jr.; Grandma and Grandpa Tomczak; Raphael Chien; R. Adaline Brunner; Paul Seegert; my publisher: Ron Whitehead; my parents: Frederick and Natalie; my brothers: Michael and Edward; my literary agent: Sidney Kramer; Peter Kopecko; my website designer: Taylor Honrath; Christian Bryant; Aunt Dottie Powers; Professor Fred Leafgren; Ruda Struhal; Jeff Stinebrink; Professor Frances Calder; Joshua Tilford; Stephanie Scott; Chris Omernick; Chris Scriven; David Schulson; Travis Sykes; Taylor Honrath; Jason Driskill, plus, Angel Blanco. And, last but not least, Arthur Rimbaud, Charles Baudelaire, Frederich Nietzsche, Sigmund Freud, and Jim Morisson, wherever they may be.

Each will know why.

You can also visit the official website of The Lost Diaries Of Jim Morrison, designed by Taylor Honrath, at www.thelostdiaries.com

Printed in the United States
1540100001B/304-309